# *Too Fast For You*

*USA Today Bestselling Author*

# **Dani Haviland**

Cover by Michele Hauf

## Book Description

Ten years after Little League, two talented professional baseball players wind up on the same minor league team. Will she remember him? And will their friendship be ruined if she does?

## NOTE:

This story takes place in two eras: Then and Now. If you look at the chapter name, you won't get confused.

# Dedication

This book is dedicated to my good friend, Gregg Frost, who took it upon himself to coach Little League teams (at one point, SEVEN teams during the same season) because there was a shortage of volunteers. His dedication to teaching young men and women both the techniques of the sport and life skills and manners helped shape hundreds of young people into better citizens, friends, and co-workers. Thanks, Coach!

# Chapter 1: Now

*Present Day*

"Yup. She's the one…" José said as he peered at the curvy young woman in a generic white baseball uniform — no team or player name visible — who was pitching to Coach in the far field, trying out for his team.

"Her? What are you talking about? I thought you were into dudes."

José glared at his minor league roommate who had joined him to spy on the unadvertised but sanctioned team tryout, but said nothing.

"What?" Felipe asked, grinning in embarrassment. "I've never seen you bring a girl to our room and you always say no to a threesome."

"You only asked me once," José said, "and she was so slutty, I was afraid I'd catch crabs from her just from being in the same hotel!"

"Yeah, well you were right about that one," Filipe said, subconsciously scratching his groin in recall. "But I asked the other guys. They said you always turned them down, too, so no one asks anymore."

José turned his back on his friend and walked up to the top row of the bleachers. He adjusted the power of his binoculars for the fifth time, hoping to get a better look at the ponytailed player. "So, just because I don't want to have relations with women of loose morals, that automatically makes me a homosexual?"

Felipe picked up his spotting scope and followed him to see 'the one' who was trying out for the Tornadoes. "Who talks like that, dude?"

"Obviously, I do."

"Hey, I know her!" Felipe said, focusing in. "That's Frosty! She's the most frigid girl to ever hang around a ball club."

José set his binoculars down and gave his own version of a frosty glare at his friend.

"What? I'm just sayin'. I mean," Felipe stammered, uncomfortable again. "There aren't many girls interested in playing baseball. Those who are only doing it because they want to find hook-ups with the guys in the major league. I mean, who wouldn't want to be the babe for someone making mega millions? Shoot, if I didn't like girls so much, I'd switch teams, if you know what I mean," he said, making a limp-wristed gesture.

"I don't care who you hang out with as long as you don't bring vermin or contagious diseases back to our place or the locker room. But you're wrong about Loren. She's committed."

"Yeah, and you should be, too. Committed, that is. I think you're nuts if you're going after her."

\*\*\*

"Gather round, guys," Coach Hanover said, and waited with clipboard in hand. When half the team ignored him, he walked up to the cluster of seasoned players gathered in front of their open lockers — chatting about their weekend — and slammed each one shut. "Come over here. Now!"

He waited impatiently, tapping his pen on the edge of his clipboard, then started over. "As you may know, Mr. Weinman and I have been going over stat sheets and videos for the last two weeks. We've finally narrowed it down and made our decision. Team, I'd like to introduce you to our newest team member. Say hello to Loren Forrest, our new first baseman and back up pitcher."

"A girl?" several of the players whispered, but no one protested above a mumble.

José stepped forward and extended his right hand. "Welcome to the Tempe Tornadoes," he said. "Your reputation precedes you. We're glad to have a player of your caliber join us." He looked around and saw the lackluster welcome by his teammates. "Aren't we, guys?" José asked, his back to Loren so she couldn't see him glowering at them.

"Yeah, yeah, welcome to the team," they said, some reluctantly, a few offering genuine welcomes after dealing with their initial shock at having a female on the team.

"I wonder what size cup she'll need," someone said.

Coach Hanover heard it and decided he'd better squash sexist comments immediately. "She won't need one, but you'll need more than a cup to salvage your career. Any — and I mean any — remarks that even come close to sexual harassment will be dealt with by an immediate suspension. And by suspension, I mean you won't play. And if you don't play, you'll be invisible to the big leagues. And if you don't play, you won't get paid either. And if you don't get paid, your wives and girlfriends just might dump you. So, I believe someone owes Forrest an apology."

"Sorry," a deep voice mumbled, its source still a mystery.

"That's better," Coach Hanover said. "Now, this is the last practice for the week. We have a big gala coming up Saturday night, though. I want everyone there, dressed in your finest and using the manners you bring out when you're trying to impress the bosses. That's what you're going to be doing, after all. Yes, we're going to introduce Forrest to the press, but it's about the team, not just her. I don't want any jealousy or other negative feelings. Show support for her. We're going to kick it this season. Spring training got off to a rotten start with Perez's broken shoulder, but I believe we can pick up where we left off. Even if you stay in the minors another year or two, it's still baseball. And if it ain't baseball, it ain't nothin', right guys, I mean gang?"

A few snorts and chuckles escaped at the word 'guys' from the group.

"Right gang?" the coach repeated.

"Yeah, yeah!" everyone said.

"All right. Keep that team spirit. Talent will only get you so far. You need that adrenaline to make it shine. Now, everyone suit up and let's go hit a few."

\*\*\*

"Well, that went well," Bubba said, holding the door to the coach's office open.

"Yeah, well, they were stunned. At least I got their initial reaction. I was afraid there'd be more resistance. I guess not. I wish there was a way I could tell if the guys had played with girls on their teams in school or Little League, but I guess it really doesn't matter. I think I can tell which guys have respect for a ballplayer regardless of gender. A few of them seemed fine with it."

"Yeah," Bubba agreed. "Looks like José either has the hots for her or he's heard about her reputation as a skilled player."

Hanover chuckled. "I'd say it's more of the reputation. Word in the locker room is he's not into girls. I don't care if he's gay, straight, transgender or a eunuch! As long as there's no grab-assin', we'll all get along fine. And I mean grab-assin' between any two players, not just men. I'm pretty sure Loren can take care of herself. She's not a newbie in playing ball with the guys. According to her dad, she insists on being just one of the team and doesn't expect any preferential treatment."

"Other than a private shower, I'm sure," Bubba said, adding a snicker.

"We'll flip a coin at the end of each game. Heads the guys shower first, tails she does."

"Sounds fair to me. And easy to remember, too."

Knock, knock.

"Hey, Coach, what drills do you want us to do first?" Felipe asked. "The guys are getting kinda antsy."

"Bring a broad on the team and they all get stupid, eh, Coach?" Bubba asked.

Hanover glared at his assistant coach, leery of berating him about his attitude in front of one of the players. He took a deep breath and decided not to play favorites here, either. "Don't ever refer to Loren Forrest — or any other female — as a broad. It's demeaning. She's just a new player. If she was a one-eye, one-horned purple player, they'd be acting just as dumb. Get over the gender slurs, Bubba. Right now!"

"Sorry," Bubba said, turning to see how Filipe was reacting to the dressing down of the team owner's son in front of one of the players.

Felipe gawked at the exchange, shocked that Coach Hanover had the balls to holler at Bubba, either alone or in front of one of the team. Shoot! The coach's career just got cut short. Real short. He'd be lucky to last until playoffs.

Filipe quickly turned around and slipped out the doorway, hoping that Bubba knew he would be discreet. He wouldn't mention it to anyone or even acknowledge that he had heard a word, especially to Bubba.

Bubba's rage was legendary. Normally easy going and the first in the group to crack a joke — usually at someone else's expense — the big guy had his father's ear. His old man owned the team and had a crew of lawyers on standby. He wasn't afraid to void a coach's or player's contract, even if his lawyers couldn't find a loophole and he had to pay off. Talk about the iron fist in the velvet glove! The guy had a razor-wire wrapped baseball bat to go with that glove! Bubba was definitely his father's son, even if the old man was making him work his way to the top of the team as a second assistant coach. At least he wasn't the go-fer.

# Chapter 2: Then

*Years and years ago*

"Wanna play?" Kyle asked the three boys hanging out around the backstop.

"With you?" Sammy shrugged a shoulder. "Maybe."

"With both of us," Kyle said, nodding to his seven-year-old sister.

"Pbbt!" Sammy blew a raspberry at the idea, then he and his minions laughed. "Why don't you go play with your dolls?"

Loren's face reddened, but she kept her cool. "Come on, Kyle."

On their way to the parking lot, a pop-up fly flew overhead, landing ten feet away. Loren picked it up and continued walking.

"Hey! That's my ball!" Sammy shouted, running in from the outfield.

"And that's your bike, right?" Loren asked pointing to the tricked-out ride that she already knew was his.

"Yeah…" the fourth-grader answered, his sprint now a cautious walk towards his classmate's little sister.

"So, how about I help you keep all your stuff together…"

Loren wound up her pitching arm with a dramatic flourish, then let a fast ball sing from her fingertips. Her dead-on delivery smacked the side of his bike's gold-flecked banana seat, knocking down the bully's top-of-the-line ride. Just as she had hoped, the titanium-framed mountain bike fell sideways and knocked down the other kids' bikes, too.

Hands on hips, she grinned widely at the success of her spontaneous release of ire with a pitch that caused a two-wheeled *clunk-thunking* chain reaction disaster.

"Come on, Loren," Kyle said, his arm around his little sister's shoulder. "We don't want to play with them anyhow."

"Yeah, they probably don't even know how to field a grounder," she said. As she turned to leave, her frustration at not being able to play caused unexpected tears to well up. She sniffed them back, not wanting anyone — even her brother — to see them. "Creeps!" she added under her breath.

After dinner, Dad listened to her story, holding her hand as she searched for words between sobs of anger. "And they wouldn't let me play just 'cause I was a girl! It's not fair!"

"I know, I know…"

"Yeah, Dad," Kyle said, "They were real jerks. It was cool when Loren threw that beaner and knocked Sammy's bike over."

"Yeah," Loren said, then giggled, wiping away her tears. "And then all his gang members' bikes fell down, too." She pulled away from her father and stood up tall, knuckles on her hips. "They dropped — bing, bang, *boom*! — just like dominoes!"

Kyle bit his bottom lip and let his sister have her healing moment, then spoke up. "Dad, they're not bad guys. They just hang out together because they don't have anyone to tell them what to do. Most of them don't have fathers. Or at least, fathers who'll spend time with them. Shoot, Sammy has the best bats and gloves money can buy, but his dad's never around to even play catch with him, much less hit a few. I never thought about it until today, but thanks for spending time with us."

"Well, we'll have to see if there's something I can do about this. Let me talk to the PE teacher at the school. It's a small town, but there still might be enough kids to start up a Little League team."

"That means girls can play, too, right?" Loren asked.

"If I have anything to do with it, dear, you can be sure I won't exclude players based on which bathroom they use. Follow the rules, show up on time, and put every bit of effort possible into playing, and any kid can be on the team. No gender bias allowed!"

"Cool!" Loren crowed, then gave her brother and dad high fives.

When the excitement settled down, Loren whispered to her dad, "But what are gender bites? I want to make sure I don't bring any and get in trouble."

"Thanks for coming in, Mr. Forrest," Mr. Anderson said. "I've asked the principal and the girls' physical education teacher to join us today. I understand you want to start up a Little League program for the kids at this school. I'm sure you already spend a lot of time with Kyle. I've watched him since you moved here last year. That kid's a natural! We could build a team around him. I'm sure…"

Craig shook his head and frowned when the boys' PE teacher got excited about having Kyle as the center of the team. "What?" the combination math teacher and coach asked. "As I said, I think he's a natural. That kid has talent…"

Craig's head continued to shake back and forth slowly. "Yes, he does, but that's not what makes a team. He'll try out just like all the other kids. He'll have to come to all the practices and run the same drills. No matter what, everyone gets treated the same."

"Oh, okay. I see. Yeah, that's a good idea. Now, as far as the girls go, Ms. Roberge has volunteered to run the girls' team. I know we have some old T-ball gear left over from a donation we received a few years ago. We don't want to leave the little ladies out now, do we?"

"Tee ball? You mean, have the girls hit a whiffle ball on a stick? No. I'm talking about having the boys and girls play on the *same* team. They'll have the same rules and responsibilities as the guys. No gender bias allowed." Craig tried to stifle his smile of pride, thinking of young women as a whole finally being able to play. "I certainly don't want to exclude some of the best players just because their plumbing is on the inside!"

"Mr. Forrest!" Ms. Roberge gasped.

The principal stifled a chuckle at the semi-graphic joke, then composed himself before he spoke up. "I don't know if folks in town will accept that, Craig. They're a conservative lot. They don't think the girls are up to it. They want their team to go to state, maybe even nationals. It's been a long time since we had anyone interested in coaching. Let's just start with the boys. If we — I mean you — get together a good team, maybe we can let one of the better girls try out for right field. After all, no one ever hits one out there, right?"

"Wrong on all counts," Craig said. He stood to leave. "I'm sorry I wasted your time."

"Wait! Wait!" the principal said, then looked back to Ms. Roberge and scowled. "Let's see if we can reach a compromise."

Craig sat back down. "What do you have? Shoot."

"Well, how about the girls having their own softball team? I mean, that is a step up from tee-ball, right?"

"Mr. Anderson, this is a small town. The pool of potential players isn't much bigger than the number of boys *and* girls between seven and thirteen. I don't see any reason to exclude anyone from trying out. If you can give me one good — and I mean *very* good — reason a girl can't throw, hit, or catch a ball as well as a boy, I'll back off."

Ms. Roberge grinned. She was unsure about this transplanted Texan when he showed up, but now she was beginning to like him. She looked at the principal and shrugged, agreeing with Craig. "It's not as if they're high school boys tackling second grade girls on a football field. Baseball's not a contact sport and all the players will be in teams determined by age. I say, 'Go for it.' And if you need an assistant coach for a co-ed team, count me in."

***

"Come on, Loren, hit it deep into center field," Kyle called, then tossed an easy pitch to his sister.

*Fwap!*

"All right!" Kyle hollered. "Only three more balls left, and then we need to bring 'em in so you can pitch to me."

"You swing like a girl!" a voice called out from the oleander bushes.

"Yeah, like a girl," other young male voices echoed.

Loren set the tip of her bat down while keeping hold of the handle. "Why, thank you!" she said, giving a quick bow. She picked it up again, set it on her shoulder, and assumed her batting stance. "Give me another one, Kyle, but don't make it so easy on me this time."

Kyle wound up his pitch, then fired off a fast ball, right through the strike zone.

*Fwap!*

Loren and Kyle both shielded the sun from their eyes as they followed the ball's arc over the fence and into the parking lot.

"And I hit like a girl, too," she said to the boys who had come out of the bushes, hoping to watch her fail.

\*\*\*

"I can't believe so many girls showed up for tryouts," Sammy said. "Don't worry, guys. The coach only cares about letting his daughter play. Loren isn't too bad, but she won't want to be the only girl. When the others don't make it, she'll drop out, too."

"Yeah, she'll drop out, too," Ray Ray echoed.

"All right, everyone," Craig said, adjusting his cap to give them a moment to settle down. "We're going to see what you have to start with. I don't expect anyone to be perfect. That's what practices are for: teaching you skills. Some of you have played catch or 'three flies and you're up,' but I'm not going to run you through that yet. We're not having tryouts today."

"Huh's?" and "Why not's?" buzzed among the kids. They finally settled down and all eyes were on the new coach.

"Becaaause," Craig said, stretching out the word, "Everyone is automatically on the team."

"Ah, man," Sammy's gang of five groaned. There were going to be girls on the team. And not just one, but six of them!

Several of the girls giggled and jumped up and down, clutching each other's hands. Most of the other students were giving each other high fives, glad they didn't have to prove themselves — or show themselves failures — in front of everyone.

But not Kyle and Loren. Both were shocked speechless. They looked at each other, stunned at their father's decision. "But…" Loren started to ask but was nudged to silence by her brother.

"Not now," he whispered. "We'll find out later."

"Settle down, everyone. Now, just because you made it on the team doesn't mean you automatically get to stay on the team all season. You have to come to every practice. Even if you break your arm falling off a bike, you have to show up. Does everyone understand?"

"Yeah's," and "Uh-huh's," were scattered around.

When their classmates had finished their lackluster acknowledgment, Loren and Kyle looked at each other, then said together, "Yes, Coach."

"Now, that's how you respond when I ask you a question or tell you to do something. I'm going to teach you a lot about baseball. Not everything I know, because that would take too long. But there's more to sports than just knowing when to swing. I insist on good manners and respect. Your chances of making it in this world by having a career in baseball — or any professional sport — is slim. No matter where you wind up, though, I can guarantee you politeness and grace will get you further than a .450 batting average."

"Yes, Coach," Loren and Kyle said, stifling their giggles. They'd heard the speech before and knew the correct response.

"I can't hear you," Craig said, looking at the rest of the group, nodding to them one by one.

"Yes, Coach," they replied, a few at a time.

"Do you want to try that again?" Craig asked.

"Yes, Coach," they chorused, a few of them laughing, the others groaning.

"Now, that's better. See, you already learned something very important today."

"When are we gonna get to batting practice?" Sammy asked.

"How about we start with raising hands to get my attention. If you didn't notice, there's a lot of us here. It can get a little crazy if everyone asks questions at the same time. I need to know names before we go any further. You may or may not know each other, so let's introduce ourselves, starting with you."

"Me?" Sammy asked, pointing to himself. *You don't know who I am? Idiot. Everyone knows my dad's the richest rancher in this part of the state, and I'm his only son!*

"Yes, you," Craig said. *I'm not going to cut you any slack just because your daddy's the richest rancher in the state!*

"It's Sammy. Sammy Silvestri."

"Well, Sammy Silvestri, if you have an ounce of talent and a gallon of determination, you might just wind up as great a hitter as that other Sammy: Sammy Sosa."

Sammy snorted with disgust, then realized everyone was staring at him, including the new coach. "Yes, sir," he said, then inhaled deeply, remembering the correct response. "Yes, Coach."

Craig went down the line, using mnemonic devices to remember their names: Sassy Sammy, Ridiculous Ray Ray, Grinning George. It was hard not to judge them by their attitudes, but he'd try. Most of them were scared. Hopefully, finding out that there wasn't any pressure to get on the team would help them focus on getting along with each other. Skills were a lot easier to teach than cooperation.

"*Señor! Señor!* I mean, sir!" a frantic woman cried out from behind the chain link fence. "Is it too late for my son to try out for the team? He's a real good player."

The woman, who bore a strong resemblance to Jennifer Lopez, was still in her maid's uniform, urging her bashful son in front of her. "His name is José Cabrera. His father, God rest his soul," she said, crossing herself, "was a baseball player in Venezuela. You see, Enriqué died before our son was born. I did the best I could to teach him *béisbol*, but we've been moving all over the country. I'm sure he'll be a good player for the team."

"Mrs. Cabrera? Hi, I'm the coach, Craig Forrest. Well, José, welcome to the team. I was just getting to know everyone's name. Oh, and congratulations!" Craig reached out and shook the reticent boy's hand. "You made it on the team!"

Craig turned to the mother. "Mrs. Cabrera, if you'd like to come sit in the bleachers, there are a few other parents here. I'm just going over the rules with the rest of the team."

"Elena," she said. "Please, call me Elena."

"All right, Elena. José, come this way."

"Oh, my!" Elena said, her hand up to cover her mouth. "You have girls playing on the same team as the boys?"

"Yes, ma'am. That isn't going to be a problem, is it? I mean, my own daughter is on the team. I treat them all the same: with respect. I expect them to treat me and each other the same way."

"Okay. I guess it's okay. Yes, yes!" Elena's eyes brightened. "I always wanted to play on a team. All I got to do was practice with my brothers, though. Yes, yes! It's very okay!"

Craig handed out copies of the practice schedule to everyone. "As you can see, we meet four days a week for drills and practice games. Now that José has joined us, we have sixteen on the team. That might seem like a lot since we only need nine, but we can break up into two teams this way. That is, if everyone stays with it. This won't be easy, but just think how great it will be when we win district."

"Or state!" Loren hollered.

"Yeah, yeah," the group cheered on.

"That's the attitude," Craig said. *Let's just hope it lasts!*

***

After two weeks, the team had thinned out to ten players. Only one other girl besides Loren had remained. The others, including one boy, decided to take the afterschool cheerleading class.

"Sorry about that," Ms. Roberge said. "I got a lot of pressure from the mothers. It wasn't so much that they didn't want their daughters to play ball, it's that the fathers wanted their girls to be cheerleaders. At least, that's what the moms said. Personally, I think those prima donnas just want to live vicariously through them — wearing short skirts and kicking their feet high in the air. Are you sure you can do without me as the assistant coach?"

"I'm sure. You go ahead and make the parents happy. I have a strong team. These guys and gals are all committed. This happens all the time. The kids dropping out, I mean; not losing players to cheerleading."

***

Craig dragged the patched equipment bag onto the field. "Okay, team. Stretch, then run three laps around the field. When you're done, we'll field some grounders."

"Dad, is there any way we can get some new bats and gloves?" Loren asked, holding up the right-handed glove that had come unlaced again. "I'm getting pretty good at re-lacing, but these gloves were rescued from the trash. I'm sure they were!"

"Well, I'm not going to argue with you there. If I had the bucks, I'd supply the team with new equipment and uniforms. This is a poor town, though. I don't think even the little grocery store has enough money to sponsor our team. I'll make a few phone calls and see what I can scrounge up. In the meantime, I'll remind the team, 'If you have it, share it.'"

"Hey, Coach!" Sammy called out, waving his hand overhead as he strutted onto the field.

"You're late," Craig said, scowling. "This is your third time."

"Yeah, I know," Sammy said, then picked up and dropped the bag he'd been pulling behind him at Craig's feet. "Sorry about that. But I had a good reason! I got the team a present. Or my dad did," he added, his eyes averting Craig's.

"Wow!" Craig said, setting the new equipment bag on end to inspect it.

"And it's got wheels, too!" Loren said.

"Look what else I got." Sammy set the bag down and started pulling out bats and gloves, balls and cans of glove oil. "I'll get us, I mean, my dad will get us uniforms when we figure out what we're going to call the team."

Craig noticed the slip. He'd bet that Sebastian Silvestri didn't have a clue about how generous he was to this poor town's Little League team. Or how happy he had made his son by *not* paying attention to him this time.

"All right, all right," Craig said. "We'll have time to sort through this after laps. Sammy, thanks for bringing it in. Next time, give me a call if you can't make it on time. I'm not gonna suspend you, but you'll have to give me an extra lap."

Sammy's face reddened, sweat glistened on his upper lip and his nostrils flared. His mouth opened, ready to protest, then shut. He took a deep breath. "Yes, Coach. Sorry I was late," he said mechanically, then dropped the bat he'd been holding, and sprinted to take his first lap. Maybe he'd outrun his anger at both the coach for punishing him, and his father for ignoring him. Maybe. But not likely.

"Hey, Dad, I mean, Coach," Loren said. "All the gloves are right-handed throw."

"Well, then, I guess it's a good thing yours is in great shape. You and José will have to keep sharing."

"Da-ad! What happens when we play a real game? We can't share a glove then!"

"Hey, Loren," José called from the pitcher's mound. "Catch!"

José threw the baseball across home plate, right-handed.

"I thought you were a lefty," Loren said.

"I guess not," José said. "It's easier to throw baseballs than oranges, though." He picked up another baseball and tossed it in the air and caught it, first with his right hand, then with his left. "Looks like you might not have to share, after all."

"Okay, everyone," Craig called out to the team, who were still pawing through the new equipment. "Sammy's got two laps on you now. Get up and take your three. We'll break into teams and if we have time after grounder practice, we can hit a few balls before it gets dark."

When Sammy got near Craig on his last pass, the coach stopped him. "Walk with me and cool down on this last one," Craig said, offering him a bottle of water.

"Sure thing, Coach," Sammy said, wiping his forehead, then accepting the drink.

"Are you sure your dad's cool with getting us uniforms? How about if we do a little fund raising with the team instead? You know, build team spirit and all that stuff. Would that be okay?"

Sammy took a cautious swallow, trying not to throw up with the image of what his father would do to him if he caught him using his charge card again. He was pretty sure he was safe this time — buying it from the same place Dad got his golf gear — but if he tried it at a uniform store, he'd probably get another trip to fist city.

"Yeah, team building's a good idea. Why didn't I think of that?" Sammy said, a wide grin of relief brightening his outlook on the day.

"Why? Because you're not the coach. One of these days, though, you'll make a good one. Looking out for others is the first step."

***

"I can't believe we won our first game!" Savannah said. "My mom is so happy! She said she didn't care if I got into her makeup or not if I'm gonna be a baseball star. Woo-hoo!"

"Don't get too wound up," Craig said. "They were playing one man short, and most of the rest of their team is still recovering from food poisoning."

"Still, it was a win, huh? They can't take that away, can they?" Savannah asked.

"Yes, it's still a win. Just know that in two days, we have a game with last year's district winners. They won't go easy on us just because we're a new team, either."

# Chapter 3: Now

*Arizona's Grandest Resort*
*March, present day, evening*

"This place is the bomb!" Felipe said as he took in the outdoor lounge and waterpark area from the balcony, the concrete and water expanse reflecting the golden glow of the palm-tree placed sodium lamps. "I wish we were staying here instead of at that discount dive by the airport. Noisy, stinky, and with the worst continental breakfast around!"

"At least, we're having the meet and greet at this place and not the ballpark," José said. "It's only March, but it was almost a hundred degrees today! I'll sure be glad when they get us set up with apartments. If we weren't due in the conference room so soon, I'd be in that water. Did you know they even have a wave pool?"

Just then, the megawatt water pumps roared into action. Most of the dozen folks still left in the rectangular pool clutched their bright yellow inner tubes and 'oohed' and 'aahed' at being carried up with the water, then gently set back down. A few of them floated flat on their backs, enjoying their buoyant ride with lips tight, making sure they kept their mouths closed so they didn't swallow pool water. Everyone, though, had contented smiles.

"Coach said there would only be adults in the apartment complex we're getting housed in next week," Felipe said. "Those carpet kangaroos at the hotel, running up and down the halls at all hours, are driving me nuts. Just as soon as I fall asleep, it's 'crash, bang, thump-thump-thump!' and I'm awake again. What's the matter with parents these days? Don't they care about their kids or manners? What happened to basic consideration?"

"I don't know…" José said as he watched the waves rise and fall. His words faded as his focus intensified. He squinted to make sure. *It's her! Doesn't she know we have to be in the reception hall in twenty minutes?*

"Yeah, well, I don't know either. Are you ready to go?" Felipe asked, as he checked out his reflection in the plate glass window, making sure his hair was slicked back and not a lock out of place.

"No, not ready yet," José said, then turned back to face him. "Go ahead without me. I'll catch up. Don't drink all the beer. I might want one, too."

"Yeah, right…" Felipe said. "I'll save *one* for you, just in case you get thirsty for something besides iced tea or water."

"Yeah, yeah. You do that," he said and spun Felipe around toward the elevators. "I'll be there in a sec."

"No doubt. I don't think you've ever been late to anything in your life!"

José waited until Felipe was in the elevator before heading back to his viewing spot. He leaned over the second-floor railing as far as he dared to verify her identity. The ponytail was unmistakable, but he never knew that Loren was hiding such a voluptuous body under her baseball uniform. *She must wear spandex to keep those beauties contained. Geez! The guys would faint if they ever saw her like this!*

Loren reacted as if a bee had stung her on her tight white belly. She flipped over suddenly and swam toward the shallow end of the pool where she could stand up and not be overwhelmed by the rolling waves. Squinting at the coconut-decorated clock underneath the cabana, she saw the time.

"Crap!" she huffed as she half-swam, half-ran out of the water to the beach chairs. She grabbed a towel and swiped it over her body as she sprinted toward the changing area.

"No running," a young girl with swim goggles on her head shouted from the pool.

"Sorry," Loren called back. "I'm late."

José watched as she paused to wrap the towel around her head, then raced across the concrete barefooted. "Ow! Ow! Ow! Damn! Damn! Damn!"

Rather than go into the conference room right away, José strolled down the pebble-embedded concrete beach lined with lounge chairs and tables. The temperature had dropped to a comfortable number, and a gentle breeze was blowing over the waves. The wind carried the scent of the chlorine-enhanced water toward him, a clean, crisp smell with a subtle hint of coconut-scented suntan lotion. Just as he was getting ready to sit down and relax in one of the beach chairs, he heard it.

*Oooh! Barracuda!*

"I know that ringtone!" José looked over and saw it on a chair four feet away. Loren's phone was sitting on a beach lounger, her sandals and sunglasses right next to it. "She'll need these sooner or later. Most likely, sooner."

José waited for Loren to come out and retrieve her goods, but when he saw he only had three minutes before the event started, he decided to go in without her. Picking up a hand towel from the shelf, he used it to wrap her belongings into a neat cylinder. He'd catch up with her later.

Again.

A smile grew. She didn't remember him from years ago or have a clue who he was. He'd get to know her all over again.

José walked in the banquet hall and scanned the room for his hotel mate. Felipe stood up and toasted him with a bottle of brew. "Hey,

José! I thought you'd never get here."

"You know me," José replied, coming over to the crowded table. "I wouldn't want to ruin my perfect record of always being on time. Looks like you saved me one," picking up the bottle with a wedge of lime in it.

"Yeah, well, we're not supposed to have more than three drinks over the whole evening. I already had mine, so maybe you can order another. I need this one." Filipe took the beer from José's hand, tossed the lime, and tipped the bottle back, chugging half of it down in one swallow. "Man, it's hot tonight."

"Not really," José said. He turned around in his seat — looking to see if they were supposed to go to the bar or were servers bringing the beer — when he saw her.

"Wow," was heard across the entire room when she walked in, her long hair still slightly moist but worn down, cascading over her shoulders like ribbons of caramel and milk chocolate.

"Sorry I'm late," Loren said, looking right at the table where Coach Hanover and Albert Weinman, the team's owner, were seated.

Bubba stood up and offered her a chair. "You're not late, Ms. Forrest," he said, looking at his watch. "You're right on time."

All eyes were on her as she accepted the seat, gracefully moving aside her long orange and yellow-flowered silk dress to sit down.

*Aha! She isn't wearing shoes! I'll just have to make sure I find a way to sit next to her for a minute.*

"May I get you a drink?" Bubba offered, his head bowed down as if he were speaking to royalty.

"Iced tea would be fine," she replied.

"No charge for mixed drinks tonight. The boss is paying for everything," Bubba said, a half-sneer sneaking out at the word 'boss.'

"I'd actually prefer iced tea. Oh, and no sweetener, please."

"Yeah, I'm sure you're sweet enough without it," Bubba said, then hiccupped. "Oops! That was a sneaky little Manhattan!"

Loren grimaced at the verification that her assistant coach — and the owner's son — had been drinking. There was only one thing worse than a drunk, and that was a drunk who was in a power position, especially a boss in two ways!

As soon as Bubba was out of sight, José moved over into his seat. "Here," he whispered to Loren, handing her the rolled-up hand towel under the table. "You forgot these by the pool."

"Wha?" she asked, then looked up and saw Bubba heading back. "Yes?" she said to the big man who was already stumbling.

"Did you want herbal or that other stuff? Um… I can't remember what they call it. Non-herbal, maybe?"

"Surprise me," she said, and flashed what she hoped was a polite but non-enticing smile. *Yup, all sorts of trouble. Lusty drunk man in power…*

"I'd ask you to join us at our table," José whispered, breaking her reflection on the possible hurricane that was brewing, "but I don't want you to upset the bigwigs. If you need a break, just look my way and nod. I'll ask you to dance or something. Not that I can dance…"

"You trying to take my girl?" Bubba sneered, a tall iced tea with a slice of lemon on the side in one hand, a Manhattan with a black cherry in the other.

Albert Weinman and Coach Hanover and everyone else within earshot froze at Bubba's declaration of ownership.

"He's joking," Loren said, and took the iced tea, and everyone but Bubba gave a sigh of relief.

"Not really," Bubba mouthed soundlessly.

No one heard him, but José had seen the lip-synched words and the possessive look in his eyes. Drunk or sober, this man was going to be trouble for Loren and the team.

# Chapter 4: Then

*Years and Years ago*
*Friday night*

"Congratulations, team! Here's to your first win!" Craig said. He held up his plastic tumbler of root beer to toast their victory. "Cheers!"

"Cheers!" the team replied, clinking glasses and spilling soda over the table's laminated surface and each other.

"Hey, Coach," Savannah called out. "How come you said it was our first win? We won last week. This is our second win."

"Not how I figure it. If we're not playing against a full squad, it's not winning. Now, if it was their nine healthy players against our nine healthy players and we won, I'd count it. Nah. Today was your first win as far as I'm concerned. And it was a great one. You all played fantastic. Now, who wants pepperoni and who wants cheese?"

José stood in the corner, watching arms fly over shoulders as team members grabbed for their favorite flavor. He wasn't too sure about whether he wanted to be a part of this group. Any group. But his mother had insisted that he learn how to play 'the American way.' It wasn't enough just to know how to catch, pitch, and hit.

'There's a real science to it,' she had said. 'A complicated logic. It's a mind game, too. You have to know when to bunt, when to steal a base, which ball to throw to the best hitters and when to walk someone. You see, an ace slugger only getting one base and bringing everyone else in is better than him hitting a home run. You'll see. I think this Mr. Forrest is going to be good for you.'

"Whatcha doin' over there, José?" Craig called out. "Come on over and get some dinner before these gluttons eat it all."

"Yes, Coach," José answered, an unexpected smile at being accepted rising. *Maybe being part of a team isn't too bad.*

After everyone had settled down, and trying to decide if polishing off the last three pieces was doable, Craig tapped the side of the plastic pitcher of root beer with his fork. *Clink! Clink! Clink!*

"Okay, everyone. Listen up. We have some business to conduct. We have to choose a name for this team." He took out the small spiral notebook he always kept in his shirt pocket and a pen. "Now, first thing we do is get suggestions. Then we'll vote. Anyone care to go first?"

"How about the Gilbert Godzillas?" Ray Ray asked.

"Godzillas?" Craig echoed. He shook his head but wrote it down. "Anyone else? We can't have a vote unless we have at least two names."

"How about the Gilbert Girls and Guys Team?" Savannah suggested.

"That should be Gilbert Guys and Girls," Sammy said, "Because there are more boys than girls."

"All right." Craig wrote both names down. "Come on, you all are more creative. How about everyone has to give me a name or you'll have to split the bill for dinner with me?"

The group came alive, abuzz with excitement as they chattered about possible team names with each other, breaking off into groups of three or four to bounce them off each other before sharing with the group.

Sammy stood up on his chair and hollered, "I think it should be the Silvestri Slammers since my dad bought all the equipment."

The roar of discussion dropped to two seconds of stunned silence, then "No's," and "No ways," were bantered about.

"I'll put it down and we can vote on that one, too," Craig said, unintentionally wincing. If Sammy's dad hadn't found out already about his 'donation' of equipment, naming the team after him would surely make him wonder why.

"Hey, Dad, I mean, Coach," Kyle said. "How about the Gilbert Gila Monsters?"

"All right. Next."

"Gilbert Gorillas!" one boy suggested.

"Arizona Artichokes!" Loren called out.

"The Best Team Ever," José shouted, almost on top of her, wanting to contribute but also hoping to stay anonymous in his recommendation.

Craig was frantically writing names down but paused at the last one. "I like that. The Best Team Ever. I've never heard of a team called that. All right, gang. If you haven't suggested a name, raise your hand and give it to me now. Otherwise, I'm going to put these to a vote."

One hand raised up. One of Sammy's minions, nicknamed Sheldon the Shy, whispered, "The Lucky Lizards."

The whole group, including Craig, groaned at the name, but it made the list.

After the vote was over, it was unanimous: The Best Team Ever.

"We have lots of practices, guys and gals, but I want you to think of ways to raise money for uniforms. Bake sales, car washes, anything you can think of, let me know. And if one or more of your parents could help, I'd appreciate it. I still have to work my day job, too, you know."

Ray Ray raised his hand. "Coach, my mom's here. Can I go now?"

Craig looked up and saw that several of the parents had arrived on time and were ready to take their kids home. "All right. Make sure you let them know about the volunteer opportunities to raise funds for our outfits."

A few of the kids said, "Huh?"

"That means we need help raising money for uniforms."

"Oh, yeah."

"Right."

Twenty minutes later, all the children had left with parents except for José. "Did you remind your mother to pick you up at 7:30?" Craig asked.

José bowed his head in shame. "Yes, but she has to work nights." He lifted his chin. "It's all right. I can walk home. She doesn't lock the door so I can get in. No problem."

"What's her number? I'll give her a call."

"No!" José said, the terror resonating in his voice. "I mean, we don't have a phone. She'd get in trouble if you called her at work. Really, it's okay. I'm home at night by myself most of the time. She gets home about midnight, so it's not as if I'm alone all night."

"Hmm. How about if you spend the night with Kyle? I can drop by your place and put a note on the door, letting your mother know where you are. I'll leave my phone number, too."

"Hey, man. It'll be fun," Kyle said. "I'll show you my baseball cards. Plus, I have a video game. It's already set up for three controllers. Dad doesn't mind backing out. You and Loren and I can play. It'll be awesome!"

José grinned at the idea of doing anything besides watching their old black and white TV or reading. "Okay."

"Cool," Loren said and gave him a high five.

"Friday night at the Forrests," Craig said. "Who knows? It could become a tradition."

***

"I still think it should have been called the Silvestri Slammers," Sammy said to his gang. "You watch, one of these days, I'm going to own my own ball team. And when I do, I'll name it whatever I want."

"Yeah! Yeah!" the guys shouted in support.

"And there won't be no stinking girls on the team, either," Sammy added, then pushed up his ball cap. "Come on, guys. Let's go find something to do. Something we'd get in trouble for if they caught us."

# Chapter 5: Now

*Arizona's Grandest Resort Ballroom*
*Present Day*

José, wary of his drunken assistant coach, slipped away from Loren's side, and in a bold voice, said, "Thanks for the tip," before he walked back to his table.

Loren shot him a quizzical look, then realized he was just making an excuse for why he had come to sit next to her. "You're welcome," she said. "Those fast balls can be tricky to catch in the field."

"Nothing's too fast for you, I'm sure," José said and winked. *Crap, dude! Why did you wink? All eyes are on you two.* José looked around the room and saw that he was only half right. All eyes were on her, not him. *Phew!*

"Okay, everyone," Coach Hanover called out from the podium. "I think the team has had their limit on the booze, so let's bring on our delicious Chicken Tetrazzini dinner…"

"Ugh…"

He paused, waiting for the groans about eating chicken to die down before continuing. "When we're done, we'll have coffee, dessert, and then some very important announcements. Oh, and in case you haven't noticed, I invited the press here tonight. You know what that means: be on your best behavior!"

"Yeah, right!" "Whoop, whoop!" and loud whistles answered the coach's light-hearted admonishment. However, his smile dropped when he saw Bubba leaning over Loren's shoulder, his nose in her hair, sniffing deeply.

"Crap!" he whispered, glad that he had moved away from the mic.

José and everyone else in the area could see what was going on, but like Coach Hanover, they didn't want to cause a scene.

"Excuse me," José said, coming up to Loren. "Your dad is on the phone. He said he couldn't get through on yours."

"I didn't hear no phone ring," Bubba slurred, then reached across Loren and put his hand on her arm, pinning it to the table so she couldn't get up.

"It was set on vibrate," José said. "I didn't want it ringing during the event. He said it's something about Kyle. I think you'd better take it."

Loren grabbed Bubba's fingers and pried them off her arm, then stood up. "José said it's my father!" she huffed to Bubba. "Otherwise, how would he have known my brother's name?"

Bubba looked up at José and sneered. "Tell her old man that she's busy. She'll call him back later."

"Let me have the phone," Loren said, then turned to Bubba. "And you…you…you *assistant* coach, don't ever touch me again!"

José ceded the phone to Loren, wide-eyed. She had barely pulled her verbal punch. His initial slack-jawed shock transitioned to a wide, contented smile of admiration at her boldness. She hadn't even been officially announced as a member of the team, yet she was already telling off Bubba. That's something just about everyone on the team had wanted to do at one time or another. And the way she glared at him with disgust when she called him assistant coach — classic!

Loren stomped out of the room with the phone to her ear — wearing her sandals, José noticed —all eyes at the table following her. "Hello? Hello?" She looked at the cellphone, then up at the faces of all the people watching her. She paused a microsecond, the wonder showing on her face, then brought the phone with no one on the other end back to her ear and smiled broadly. *What a clever ploy, José.*

"Oh, hi, Dad. Oh, I'm okay. I forgot my phone. I thought I told you we were having a fancy dinner tonight. Okay. I'll see if José can take some pictures for you. He's a peach! I'll call you later. Bye!"

This time, Loren was composed and all smiles, her face brilliant at being saved by the dark-haired Hispanic player who didn't say much. A few of the guys had let her know she didn't have to worry about him hitting on her because he was gay. Cool. She could use a friend who wasn't looking for benefits. This minor league stuff might not be too scary after all!

"Here's your phone, José," she said, handing it back to him, patting his hand in appreciation. "Thanks."

"Anytime. You can sit here if you'd like," he said, then nodded towards Bubba.

Coach Hanover was standing over the seated drunk, his hand heavy on Bubba's shoulder, keeping him from standing up or leaving as he gave him a stern lecture at low volume. The others at the table were definitely getting an earful, but they were all in the inner circle. Who were they going to tell? Besides, they already knew about the owner's son's problems.

José chuckled. "It's less exciting over here, if you know what I mean. But you're welcome to join us."

Loren rolled her eyes, then moved her long skirt aside to sit down. "I guess I can get my phone back later."

"Yeah, when Bubba's gone," José said.

Felipe chimed in, "Yeah, maybe this time for good."

Dinner was served, the players at Loren's table all getting along as if they had played together for years. Felipe was slightly sloshed but had become enamored of one of the servers, a cute brunette with a smile that was only outshone by her wiggle.

"Are we allowed to tip the servers?" he asked when she set his cheesecake in front of him.

"No, but you are allowed to date them," she said, winking as she handed him a slip of paper with her phone number. "I'm off work at ten."

"See if you can make it nine-thirty. Curfew's at ten."

"Woo!" she squealed as he slyly squeezed her bottom. She leaned over his other shoulder and whispered, "Hurry up nine-thirty!"

Ten minutes later, Coach Hanover was at the podium again, a miniature gong and mallet held up for everyone to see. "Is everyone ready for the news?" he asked.

The crowd continued to murmur over dinner, some of the conversations so loud they almost sounded amplified.

"Okay, you asked for it," he said, then held the black frame with the hanging bronze disc in front of the mic. He struck it with the miniature mallet.

*Gong!*

All the attendants ceased talking and turned toward the dais.

"All right, then," Coach said. "Now that I have your attention…"

"Just don't bring that to the games," a voice called out.

"Hey, I'm the coach," he said. "I can do whatever I want."

"Unless the owner says no," Bubba called out.

Coach Hanover's jaws clenched, but he forced a smile. "That's correct. Now, I have two major announcements to make. First, I'd like to welcome our newest teammate. As a few of you already know —as in, everyone in the Tempe Tornadoes ball club — we are welcoming the first female pitcher and first baseman in the minor leagues. I don't think we'll have her around too long, though."

Whispers of "Why?" and "Huh?" and "What's he talking about?" rumbled across the conference room.

The coach took a deep breath and waited for the hubbub to die down. "I say that she won't be around the Tempe Tornadoes for long because I'm sure that when our guys in the majors see how great she can perform; she'll be called up in a hurry. Oh, and just so there's no confusion, her fantastic ball playing skills have nothing to do with her gender. Here she is, folks: Loren Forrest! Loren, come up and say a few words."

Loren leaned over and whispered in José's ear, "I'm sure glad you brought me my sandals," then stood up and looked around the room before proceeding to the podium.

"I'll say one thing, Ms. Forrest," Coach Hanover said, "There's one thing you can do better than anyone else in this club. I doubt any of your teammates would look as good in a dress."

"You haven't seen José in one yet," a voice from the back called out.

José looked around the room, trying to see without standing up and looking like a fool, who had yelled it out. Rather than succumb to the taunt, he decided to run with it. "That's just cause your legs aren't as pretty as mine," he said aloud.

The audience roared at the joke, allowing Loren a minute to make it to the podium. When the remarks and laughs died down, she said, "I think we all know that dresses don't make a ball team. And this amazing club is why we're all here tonight. I appreciate everyone's faith that I can help us win the championship this year. And that's the bottom line: I can *help*. We're a team and we will work together to make the Tempe Tornadoes the best minor league franchise ever."

Whistles and vigorous applause segued to a standing ovation, allowing Loren to graciously nod in appreciation, then make her way back to the table.

Coach Hanover came back to the mic, beaming broadly at her grace in acknowledging the team, taking all the focus off herself. He clapped again, then pointed to her. "We need more like her. And I'm not talking about women, either. Such an inspired player. Let's go, Tornadoes!"

Another round of whistles and applause brought the spirit of the group to an even higher level. The coach waited for it to die down naturally before delivering the bad news.

"All right, all right. We'd better finish up here before these folks kick us out." He looked down at his watch. "And besides, only an hour to go before curfew."

The expected groans waved across the room but quickly stopped when Coach held up his mini gong and mallet. "I think I'm in love with this little gem," he said. "So, now that I have your attention. Again. I have to give you an update. As some of you may have heard through the rumor mill, the team has an interested buyer. I'm here to clarify one misconception. This team is *not* in any kind of financial trouble. A person or corporation — sometimes considered the same thing — has made an offer to buy the team. Normally, something like this comes with conditions. Well, if it did, I wasn't privy to the terms. Just know that, depending on how negotiations go, you might have a new owner."

"Does that mean all of us go with the deal?" a player called out.

"Generally," Coach clarified, "the team is accepted in its entirety. However, if a player is not playing up to his — or her — ability or has not abided by team rules such as disobeying curfew or appearing in public in a way that reflects poorly on the team, then he or she could be let go."

"Does that pertain to the coaches, too?" Felipe asked.

Coach Hanover gave a chagrined smirk, quickly looked over at Bubba's table, then back at Felipe. "Yes, it does. We are today, tomorrow, and forever as long as we're under contract, a team: coaches and players."

# Chapter 6: Then

*After the pizza party*

"Are you sure this is the best place to put your note?" Craig asked, his hand hovering above the empty coffee carafe.

"Yes, Coach, I'm sure. The first thing she does when she comes home is set up coffee for the morning."

"She gets home at midnight?" he asked, although he knew that's what José had said.

"Yes, sir. That's when she gets home from her night job. She has another job that starts at six in the morning."

"She can't do that!" Craig exclaimed, then took it down a notch. "When does she sleep?"

"Her morning job only lasts until noon. She comes home and takes a nap before the night job. That's when we eat dinner together. She's a good cook. You should come by sometime. I think you'd like her."

"I met her briefly, José, and yes, I like her. Not every mother would do so much, working two jobs and still managing to make sure she and her son eat dinner together. Plus, she took you to try out for Little League."

"Yeah, well, I think we'd better get going," José said, feeling embarrassed. "I don't think Kyle and Loren want to wait in the car too long. Kyle's dying to show me that game he got."

"Okay, come on. Do you have everything you need?"

José held up his plastic bag with pajamas, toothbrush, and a change of clothes. "Yes, sir. I'm ready."

\*\*\*

"All right, gang," Craig said, setting out the ground rules for the evening. "You get to play until 10:30. Then it's lights out."

"Ah, Dad. Can't we stay up 'til midnight?" Kyle asked.

"Yeah, we don't have school tomorrow. And there's nothing to do in the morning. I mean, no chores or anything."

"You're right," Craig said. "The rain got you out of mowing the lawn for a day, at least. Let's see how well you get along before extending the mandatory bedtime. No bickering or arguing about who's turn it is, all right?"

"We got this, Dad," Kyle said, adding a wink. "We're gonna find out who's the faster pitcher, José or me."

"The fastest pitcher," Loren corrected. "And that would be me."

Craig rolled his eyes. "Just keep it down to a low roar. I want to finish this book," he said, holding up the latest mystery novel by his favorite author.

"Yeah, yeah," Kyle said. "Maybe you'll be done by my birthday. Every time you try and read that one, it puts you to sleep. You've been working on it for two months. It should be called Ellery King's Best Bedtime Stories Ever!"

"Well, maybe you're right. Either way, I'm going to work on it. I'm bushed! I wish I had your energy, guys."

"You did," Loren said. "When you were our age. Then again, we only have to deal with school and baseball. You're doing a great job, Dad. Not many men would take on raising two kids by himself and coaching a Little League team."

"And running a one-man business," Kyle said, patting his dad on the shoulder. "Don't worry, Dad. As soon as you'll let me, I'll help you. I figure maybe a year or two."

"Two?" Craig squeaked. "You're a sharp kid, but you're only eleven. I think your voice needs to be a little lower before customers will trust you for phone orders."

"Maybe. But I'll bet that pretty soon, we'll be getting lots of online orders. Don't worry. I won't let us go broke."

"Son, going broke isn't your concern; going to school and making friends is."

"And playing baseball!" Loren piped in.

"And playing baseball," Craig agreed. "Now, good night. I'll just leave it at don't stay up too late. I have a box of baking mix and a pound of bacon. We're having a big breakfast tomorrow. And if you snooze, I'll eat your portion."

"Ugh…" Loren and Kyle groaned at the same time, then hugged their dad goodnight.

Greg saw the glazed-over look on José's face and realized that the boy probably never had any family time like this. "Thanks for coming over tonight, José," he said and gave the boy a one-armed hug across the shoulders. "The more the merrier — up to a point — with a sleepover. Don't beat their numbers too bad on that video game because if you do, they'll keep you up until tomorrow trying to best your score!"

"Yes, Coach," José said, a smile of embarrassment blooming at getting an adult man's complete attention on a family level. "I'll be easy on them."

"Where'd you put the bat, Kyle?" Loren asked, looking behind the couch and recliner.

"Here," he said, and reached into the hall closet. "Catch."

Loren caught the wooden bat, then the boys grasped it, one at a time, her hand reaching over theirs to see who would be at the top and get first crack at the game. "You go first, José," she said.

"How about someone else does. I don't know how to play this one."

"Oh, but you do," Kyle said, placing the game controller strap over José's wrist. "Just hold this like a bat and swing when the ball comes at you. It's baseball without the bugs and heat!"

José took a trial swing, watching the avatar Loren had created for him move the bat in an odd arc. "That's not how you swing a bat!" she said. "Pretend it's the real deal, stance and all."

*Fwap!*

"It sounds like a real ball being hit!" José said.

"Run the bases!" Kyle said.

"Huh?"

"Run in place, just like you're on a treadmill," Loren said.

José ran in place and watched.

"See!" She pointed at his avatar, running toward first. "But don't slide. That doesn't work."

"Yeah," Kyle said. "I know it's tempting, but I broke a lamp the first — and only — time I tried that."

The three played baseball, then segued into soccer and golf before deciding to take a break. "Who wants ice cream?" Loren asked.

"Oh, yeah…" Kyle said. "Chocolate Suicide, my favorite."

"That just means more vanilla for me," Loren said. "What kind do you want, José? Pale or dark?"

"I'll go with vanilla, too. Chocolate makes me fall asleep."

Kyle looked at the clock on the microwave. "Maybe we'd better have just a little ice cream. It's already one o'clock. I want to save room for pancakes and bacon in the morning."

"You guys sure eat good stuff," José said, digging into the bowl of vanilla Loren set in front of him.

"That's only 'cause Dad likes to eat it, too. I sure hope he doesn't go on a health kick like some of the parents. I guess it's okay not to have a mom sometimes. Dads like junk food better." Kyle blanched at his remark, remembering that as far as anyone knew, José didn't have a father.

"I wouldn't know," he said, suddenly not interested in the ice cream.

"Hey," Loren said, picking up her bowl and moving next to him at the kitchen counter. "Moms and dads come and go suddenly sometimes. Ours went suddenly. We just hope that the next one will come into our lives just as fast. Who knows, maybe you'll get a dad quick, too."

"Yeah," José said, remembering the man his mother had dated two years ago. "As long as he likes kids, I guess that's okay."

"Well, I know our dad wouldn't want a wife who didn't want us, too. I don't know your mom, but I bet she'd be the same way," she said.

"Yeah, you're right. There was one guy, but when he said I'd be better off with my grandparents, Mom told him that I was here before he was. He could accept me or hit the road."

"And he hit the road, right?" Loren asked.

"Yeah," José replied, then decided he was hungry again and dug in. "My mom's pretty smart that way."

"Our dad, too," Loren said. "I guess we all got lucky with getting the right parent."

***

"This is our twelfth game, guys," Craig said. "After this one, we go to tournament. Whether it's the first, last, or a practice game, always play your best. You never know who's watching you."

"Yes, Coach," the team responded dismally, hearing the same spiel.

"I'm serious. The same goes for whatever you do. You never know. It might be a potential boss in the stands or maybe that sweet girl in your math class is watching from behind the bushes…"

"Hey, Sammy," the kids teased, causing the right fielder to blush.

"Ahem," Craig interrupted. "Let's give the cheer, then go out there and win this thing!"

"One, two, three, four! We're the Best Team Ever more!"

"I still think we should have come up with a better name," groused Sammy. "When I have my own team…"

"Yeah, yeah, yeah," Ray Ray mumbled, making sure he said it soft enough that Sammy didn't hear him.

The team went to the dugout and waited for the lineup to be read. "Sammy, you lead, then Kyle, José, and then Loren."

"Ah, Coach," Ray Ray said. "How come she has cleanup again?"

Craig flipped up the pages on his clipboard. "Do you want me to tell you your batting averages? I can do that, but I think most of you know where you are, more or less. I'm going strictly by the numbers here. I don't want to be accused of favoritism just because she's my daughter. Don't worry. Remember, we have six innings. You'll get your turn at bat, no matter how great or poorly we play."

"Yes, Coach," the team chorused.

Craig watched José when he was on deck. As always, he was searching the stands for his mother, trying not to be obvious, but he wasn't fooling anyone.

"She's not here," Sammy called out caustically.

"Yeah, and neither's your old man," José replied, then swung at the empty air, imagining Sammy's head as the target.

"Knock off the personal chatter," Craig said. "Keep focused on the game. That's all that counts until the ump calls it."

"Yes, Coach," they all said.

The bottom of the fifth inning came and went in a hurry. It was three up, three out on the other team. Loren was on a hot streak. Not one person got on base. Now it was her turn at bat.

"Hey, batter, batter, batter, swing!" they called out as Loren took her stance at bat.

*Zing!*

"Ow!" Loren yelped as the wild ball hit her in the upper left arm. "He did that on purpose!"

"Sorry!" the pitcher called out, his eyes shifting back and forth between the ump and his coach.

Craig saw the other coach's smile sneak out before disappearing under a scowl of concern. "Are you all right, miss?" he asked.

"I'm Loren," she said harshly, grasping her arm, trying to keep the sobs from following the tears that had sneaked out on their own. "And no, I'm not all right. He did that on purpose. I know it. I saw him sneer at me before he threw the ball. He just wanted to keep me from throwing my first perfect game!"

"Now, now, honey," Craig soothed, then looked up and glared at the other coach. "We need to get you to the emergency clinic. He might have broken a bone. I'm calling the game. With Loren out, we still have enough players, but we don't have a coach."

"I'll take her to the hospital," a woman's voice called out.

"Mom?" José said.

"*Sí,*" she said. "I was hoping to watch you play today."

"Here," Craig said, fishing in his pocket for his keys. "And here's her medical card, too. It's the white Ford over there. Loren knows which one. I'll catch a ride over there when we're done. I'm sure Coach Farnsworth will give me a lift, won't you?" he asked, scowling at the other team's coach.

"Oh, yeah. Sure. Do you trust her with Loren?" the portly contractor playing coach asked.

Craig looked at Elena, who was fawning over Loren, gently pushing a wayward strand of hair out of the young girl's face and offering soft words of encouragement. "She's got this. I'm not worried about either one of them, so you shouldn't be either." He looked over at them. "Elena, thanks for doing this. I'll be over there probably before the doctor has a chance to see her."

"*Sí,*" she replied, flashing the keys. "Thanks for trusting me."

"*Sí,*" Craig replied. "Okay. Let's get back to the game. Savannah, you're up. Keep a cool head and make it count."

Savannah hit a single, then the others came up and either got on base by getting a hit or being walked.

"A little shook up there, eh?" Sammy called out to the pitcher. "You'd better watch it. Payback's a bitch."

"Hey, hey," Craig scolded. "None of that trash talk. The best payback is winning, all right?"

"Yes, Coach," Sammy said, then tapped the end of the bat on the plate twice. "Right here. If you can…"

*Fwap!*

Sammy hit his first home run ever and drove in the loaded bases.

"Hold on there, Ray Ray," Craig said, holding up his hand, noticing Coach Farnsworth coming his way.

"You got us by ten runs," Farnsworth said. "I'm sure you want to check on your daughter. Let's call it a game." He stuck out his hand to shake Craig's. "Well played. And sorry about your daughter's injury. I hope nothing's broken."

Craig saw sincerity in the coach's eyes and heard it in his voice. There was no doubt in his mind that the man had hoped for — and maybe even mentioned taking out Loren with — a bean ball, but he had genuine remorse. "Ump?" he called to the umpire who was standing behind Farnsworth.

"All right, gang. I'm calling it: ten to zip. The Best Team Ever wins this one, the final game of the regular season. Enjoy the tournament if you're in it," he said, then started pulling off Velcro bindings as he walked away.

The two teams lined up opposite each other. "Good game, good game," they said without enthusiasm, as they walked past each other, giving the familiar hand slaps and high fives to enforce the good sportsman behavior that today was hard to find.

"Turds," Sammy said when they were putting up their gear.

"Yeah, I agree," Kyle said. "Sammy, thanks for keeping your cool. I know I wanted to run up there and rip off his arm and beat him with it."

"I woulda helped you if I thought we could get away with it," Sammy replied.

"Yeah, yeah," Ray Ray and Sheldon echoed.

"Kyle, let's go," Craig said, pushing the last of the bats into the equipment bag. He grabbed the handle, ready to haul it away. "Thanks for not exploding on me, guys. I know, it's one of the hardest things to do in the world. I guess that's what separates us from wild animals."

"Rowl!" Savannah snarled, and Craig and the rest of the team cracked up.

"Tell Loren I get to sign her cast first if she has a broken arm," Sammy said.

"You like her," Ray Ray teased, then backed away so he didn't get punched.

"Do not!" Sammy said.

"Do, too!" Ray Ray said, giggling.

"We all like Loren," Craig said. "Now, find your rides home so I can get out of here. Kyle, José, you're coming with Coach Farnsworth and me."

"Thanks, Coach," José said, then offered to take the equipment bag. "I got this," he said, and headed to the truck where Farnsworth was waiting.

***

"Dad, it doesn't hurt too much anymore," Loren said. "Elena had an ice pack in her lunch box and she wrapped it in a cloth. See?"

"Oh, man," Craig said, inspecting the first aid. "That's gotta hurt, ice or no ice." He ran his fingers up the length of her upper arm bone. "It doesn't feel like a break, but we'd better make sure it isn't cracked or chipped."

"They already looked. No break, just a bad bruise. I just have to take it easy for a while. I guess I won't be pitching for the tournament."

"Let it heal. The guys will be happy to rotate positions. As long as no one else gets on the injured list or joins the cheerleading squad, we'll be fine."

Elena remained seated next to José in the waiting room, both of them listening to the chatter of the concerned father. "Do you need help with anything else?" she asked.

"Oh, no. We're fine. Let me take you two out to dinner. I don't think I can stand another night of hot dogs or fish sticks."

"Ew," Loren and Kyle chorused.

"And I think they feel the same way."

"Pizza?" Kyle asked.

"Nah. I was thinking about the All You Can Eat Buffet downtown. I can't decide if I want Italian, Mexican, or Chinese, but I do know I want to start it all with a big salad. Is everyone game?"

"Mom, can we go, or do you have to go back to work too soon?" José asked.

"We can go," she said, her slight frown of disappointment overtaken by a smile of reckless abandonment. "*Sí,* let's fiesta!"

"*Sí,* let's fiesta!" they all said.

After they ate dinner, Craig gave Kyle a ten-dollar bill. "Go get some tokens and you guys can play arcade games until you run out."

"Okay, but we're pretty good at getting free games," Kyle said. "We might close the place down!"

"You won't," Loren said, "but I might. I've got the fastest hands in the west, bum arm or not."

"Don't work it too hard, Loren," Craig said. "Why don't you play The Claw and let them play the two-handed games."

"Okay. I can always be the coach. José has undiscovered skills, I'm sure," she said.

José laughed. "You'd better watch closely," he said. "I'm too fast for you."

"Not too fast that I won't see your mess-ups," she countered.

"Just have fun and please, no more trips to the urgent care, all right?"

"Yes, Dad," Loren and Kyle said.

"Yes, Coach," José added, wishing he had a dad that cool. *Maybe one of these days…*

"You have a great son," Craig said when the kids were out of earshot. "Wonderful manners and very talented, too. You said his father was a ball player?"

Elena smiled at the praise, then bit her bottom lip at the mention of his father.

"Oh, I'm sorry," Craig said, seeing her discomfort.

She shook her head, then smiled at him and said, "If I tell you a secret, would you promise not to tell anyone?"

"Sure. Shoot."

"His father was a *bandido,* a crook. I have been hiding from him since before José was born. We were never married. I tried to hide the pregnancy, escape to America before it was too late. I made it here, but I have had to move many times. I try to live in one place no longer than two years. I'm afraid it's almost time for us to move again. I'll tell José later. I don't want to spoil tonight. Thank you for dinner and the video games. He likes your son and daughter so much."

Craig was wide-eyed at her story, then paused and stared at her.

"But, wait. Where did José learn how to hit and throw? You?"

"*Sí.* I played ball with my brothers in Jalisco. They were very good, so I had to be, too. They played on the local team. One year, all three of them at once."

"I always knew there was something else about you I liked," Craig said, placing his hand on top of hers, making sure the children didn't see the familiar gesture. "If there's something I can do…" His eyes brightened with a smile. "We could get married. You'd have a different name, a different home. You wouldn't have to worry about being an illegal, either. No one would look twice at us. I'm about as gringo as they get!"

She shook her head and frowned, her despair at the situation unmistakable. "He'd find me. He always does."

Craig shifted in his seat, uncomfortable with the way the conversation had ended. They'd spent enough time together that he knew she couldn't be persuaded to do something she didn't want to do. Risking discovery by staying put, even as an American citizen with a new name, wasn't an option for her. Deep down, he had known that the afternoon lunches that had transitioned into passion-filled trysts were too good to last. She was perfect in so many ways, but if she was determined to disappear, holding onto her would only drive her away faster, further, maybe forever. He'd have to give her what she wanted and pray that eventually they'd find each other again.

Elena heard the children hollering about the video game and looked their way, a tender smile of hope at a future that included all of them quickly disappearing with the reality of her situation. "I wish we could be together…" she said, then shook her head again.

As Loren headed toward them, Craig switched emotions and attitudes, lifting his posture from the slumped shoulders of a defeated lover who had lost his woman to the straight back and wide grin of a proud father of two hardworking and driven children. "You're welcome for dinner and the entertainment, Elena. We were due for a celebration with all of us together. I just got a new contract, so I won't be scrambling so hard to make ends meet."

"Thank you for being so good to my son. He was sad all the time until he started playing baseball on your team. All week, he looks forward to spending Friday night with Kyle and Loren."

"Hey, Dad," Loren said. "Look what I got!" She held up a big Betty Boop plush doll. "The guys are on their last games. They decided to try The Claw, too, but only wound up wasting their tokens. Come on. Let's see who's got the faster hands: Kyle or José."

"José," Elena whispered to Craig as they walked into the arcade area, then winked.

"Kyle," Craig whispered back and returned the wink, his hand gentle on her shoulder to guide her to where the boys were.

"Oh, my," Loren said, then turned away, seeing the affectionate touch. She didn't have to worry about them hearing her remark, though. Not only was the area abuzz with the clanking of games and shouts of game players, the parental couple was oblivious to anyone but each other. "Oh, my," she repeated.

# Chapter 7: Now

*Behind the Resort*
*Trash bin area*

"Hey, Bubba," the deep voice called out from beside the dumpster. "How's the dumbest man to ever bet on the ponies?"

"Shit, man!" Bubba squeaked as he grabbed his dick and tried to shove it back in his pants, pissing over both hands as he tried. "What are you doing here?"

"Checking on my investment," Paco said. He watched as Bubba zipped up, then wiped his hands on the back of his dress trousers. "You're getting a little sloppy there, Ass Coach."

"Don't call me that," Bubba hissed.

Paco took two steps forward and grabbed Bubba by his loosened necktie. "I'll call you whatever I want, Ass. Coach," he repeated. "You have a lot laying on the line. You told the boss that it was a sure thing, inheriting the team from Daddy. Well, guess what? Word on the street is Daddy really ain't sick. He just spread the rumor himself to find out who his friends were and who was out to profit from his good nature. Looks like you're going to be owing a lot of bucks to De Luca if the old man sells to someone else. I mean, what good does it do if we knock off Daddy if he doesn't own the team?"

"He…he…he's not going to sell it. That's just a story he made up to get us in the headlines. If folks think there's a chance that we're moving to another town, the attendance goes up like a Fourth of July Roman candle."

Paco paused to take in what Bubba had said. It sounded logical, but his sources said otherwise. "Just make sure he doesn't sell it to anyone in the next week. And De Luca's still waiting on you for a copy of the will, naming you sole heir to the team. If you don't show it quick, he'll cut his losses — and your body into itty bitty geometric pieces. He told me he misses the old days, bein' his papa's enforcer. Still has his old tool kit, too. Said it needed cleaning up, but then again, no need to worry about you gettin' an infection if you're gonna be a wall decoration, right?"

Bubba gulped, then realized fear had squeezed out a little more pee. "I'll do my best," he said.

"Your best better be what De Luca wants or it doesn't matter if you tried or not." Paco sniffed the air, then groaned in disgust. "Go clean yourself up. You smell like shit."

\*\*\*

"Mama? What are you doing here?" José asked when he came out of his room and saw her walking down the hallway at his hotel, looking at door numbers.

"I came to watch you play," she said matter-of-factly, then reached up to kiss him on the cheek.

"But you can't be in the country. If ICE catches you, you'll get jail time."

"Then so be it. You've been playing with the Tempe Tornadoes for a year and I've never been able to watch you. It's time."

"What about the De Lucas? Do they know you're here?"

"Don't you worry about them," Elena said, scowling. She resisted the urge to spit, only because they were indoors. "*Putos*," she hissed.

"Yeah, well those *putos* would just as soon see you dead," José said. "I wish you had never told me I was related to them. They should be in prison for what they did to you."

"I was young and stupid and somewhat at fault. He should know by now that you have no interest in the family business. He is just mad because I left. It is an insult to his *machismo."*

"Mama, there is no *just* with a man like that…"

"He's a pig."

"Maybe so, but he's a pig with a gun and a knife with a lot of bad dudes working for him."

"Ahh," Elena said, patting him on the cheek. "You sound so much like an American now. Dudes. You say it so cute."

José frowned and issued a guttural growl as he took her hand from his cheek. "I *am* an American. Just because I was born of a woman from Mexico and in a border town doesn't make me less of one. Now, I have a game tonight. Please, stay out of sight. Oh, and if you happen to see anyone we know, please don't let them know who you are."

"Okay," she said, carefully enunciating the gringo word. "I sound like I was born here, too, right?"

"Yes, Mama." He gave her a hug and a kiss on the top of the head. "Now, go be invisible, *está bien?*"

"Okay," she said, smiling with pride. "You look so nice in your uniform. You make your mama proud. Now, I go and be invisible."

*** 

"Is everybody here?" Coach Hanover asked, looking around the room.

"Sorry I'm late, Coach," José said, breathless from running across the parking lot.

"And where's Forrest? Don't tell me you two are an item," he said, then laughed.

Everyone but Felipe laughed with the coach until José cut his eyes to his friend, reminding him he'd like to keep up the ruse, then he laughed, too. "You and Forresty? What a pair!" he said just a little too loud and boisterous.

"All right, all right," Hanover said, then looked at his watch. "I guess I jumped the gun. She has ten more minutes. Now, I have the lineup here. This is Loren's big debut, but I don't want to make her the star of the team. I wouldn't doubt that she's in the crapper right now, puking her guts out. I know I did my first game. She'd better get it all out now. Nothing's worse than soiling your shoes in front of a packed stadium."

"Packed?" Loren asked as she strode in. She took a deep breath and scanned the room, refusing to let anyone — especially her coach and teammates — intimidate her. "I didn't look. Everyone ready for tonight? I hear it's supposed to be a full moon. You know what they say about that, don't you? The *crazies* will be out." She ended the first act of her dramatic production with the bug-eyed glare and thumb-in-ears finger wiggles of a campfire storyteller.

José watched her from behind his locker door, a smile of pride rising at her ability to take a terrifying situation and turn it into a joke.

She walked over to her locker, a few feet away from him. "Hey, there," she said when she saw him.

"Hey," he replied. He closed the door then put his foot on the bench in front of him, retying his shoes. "You're doing great," he whispered to her.

"I'm scared shitless," she whispered back, then looked over at the team and said at full volume, "What's a gal gotta do to get a drink around here?"

Felipe put a water bottle in her hand. "Just ask," he said and winked. "You're doing great," he whispered.

"Why do people keep saying that?" she asked José when Felipe was gone.

"Because we all had first night jitters at one time, too," he said. "I'm just impressed that you're handling it better than anyone I've ever seen. Or myself. I couldn't sleep for two days before my first game. Then it was two more days before the adrenaline rush was over and I could crash!"

"Really?" Loren asked. "Gee. And I thought I was the only one."

"I'll tell you what you need to do…"

"Too late," she interrupted. "I already missed two nights sleep."

"No, I mean for tonight and tomorrow. Go to the pool — after it's closed and when no one else is there — and float. Just kick back, arms out like a water angel, and float. You can't sleep if you're tense. And because you sink if you're tense, you wind up forcing your body to relax enough to float. After that, you should be able to sleep."

"Really?" she repeated.

"Yeah, but just know that at some point, you'll dunk yourself, especially if you roll over in your sleep," José said, laughing.

"Well, maybe I'll need a spotter, then."

"Maybe," he said, then turned away and took a deep breath. *Don't think of her as a woman in a bikini, floating in a pool with only you for company. Wrong focus for a game night! At least, a baseball game night!*

"Who's the starting pitcher tonight?" the chubby-cheeked middle-aged reporter asked.

"Who said you could come in?" Coach Hanover asked.

"I didn't see any signs that said, 'No Reporters Allowed.'"

"No," the coach said, "but it did say team only, so scram!"

"Is Loren going to start tonight?" he asked, then ducked under the coach's outstretched arm and bulldozed his way through to the other players, his cameraman a scant foot behind him. "Is it true they call you Frosty?" he asked.

"What's true is that it says, 'Team Only' on the door," Loren said. She looked him up and down, an exaggerated frown on her face, totally aware that this was probably a live news feed by the grin on the TV crew's faces and the little red light on the camera. She poked the reporter in the belly, waited for him to look down, then flipped her index finger up and tapped him on the end of the nose. "And you're in no shape to be on the Tempe Tornadoes."

The reporter's face turned scarlet as he sputtered at her finger-popping him on the nose. "And that's all we have from the locker room tonight, viewers. Stay tuned for the game. And now, back to you, Deborah." He swiped his hand across his neck, indicating 'cut' to the cameraman.

"Why, you insolent bit…"

"Whoa! Whoa! Whoa there, Bud," Coach Hanover said, stepping in between the reporter and Loren before one of his team could. "You watch your mouth in here. As far as I'm concerned, you're *persona non grata* around here. Maybe your Miss Deborah at the sports desk has better manners than you. Why don't you go back and read the teleprompter and let her do the field work?"

"Well, I never…" he sputtered.

"And you never will," the coach said, his hand on the blustering man's elbow, ushering him out of the locker room, the cameraman shuffling behind him, wide-eyed at the new-to-him domain.

"Bye," the cameraman said, then looked at Loren. "Nice meeting you."

As soon as he was out of the locker room, the whole team burst out laughing.

"I think you have your first fan," one of the guys said to her.

"Yeah, well, I never expected anything like that for tension release," Loren said. "Everyone here ready to play ball?"

"You betcha," and "Hell yeah!" and, "All right!" resounded around the room.

The coach came back in the room, dusting off his hands. "Now that I have the garbage taken out, let's play ball. Loren, you're starting tonight. Might as well give them what they spent their money for."

"Yeah, they'll boo us until she comes out anyhow," one of the second-string players said.

"Well, at least they're not waiting to see you fail," Loren said, then laughed nervously.

"Just think of it as one of those Little League games you played where the other team had to forfeit because not enough players showed up, but you went ahead and played anyhow. You've already won the game, Loren. You made it this far. Just go out and have fun," José said, then smacked her on the back, just like he would one of the guys. "It all pays the same whether you stress or not."

"Thanks," she said, punching him in the upper arm. "I needed that."

***

Loren waited for the cheers, jeers, and whistles to die down before she threw the first pitch. It was right over base. "Stee-rike one!" the ump called.

The tall black pinch-hitter tapped his bat on the ground, stomped his feet a few times, and took another practice swing. Loren watched her catcher, nodding that she understood to throw a curve ball.

"Stee-rike two!" the ump hollered.

The catcher signaled to throw another curve ball. Instinct told her that this hitter was going to be a problem. After all, he didn't play the field. He made his living hitting the ball and reading pitchers. Okay. Time to play dirty. She shook her head minimally, then lifted her glove up and moved it across the front of her face, as if she was shooing a fly or a gnat.

The hitter changed his stance, ready for the fast ball he knew was in her repertoire. *She's just a girl. Overblown publicity gimmick. So easy to read, too. She's a fad that'll be over before she catches on.*

Loren wound up the pitch and let it fly. Her curve ball...

*Tink!*

The catcher stood up, walked forward and waited for the foul ball to fall right into his glove. He looked at the batter and grinned.

"You're out!" the ump shouted, his thumb pointing behind him.

No one said a word. They didn't have to. All the team members whistled and cheered but knew that they couldn't make her feel any better than she already did.

What a way to start the game!

There were ups and downs for the next six innings. Gone were the days of three up, three down on batters. Some of these guys were tricky. *Give yourself some time, Loren. Halfway through the season, you'll know everyone's tells.*

At the top of the seventh inning, Coach Hanover pulled Loren aside. "That was a great start for your career, Forrest. I normally don't let first time pitchers go that many innings, but you didn't show you were tiring. Plus, the fans are eating it up. I want to save some for the next games, though. I'm letting Sanderson pitch the rest of the game."

Loren gave a wide toothy smile, her relief apparent to everyone. "Thanks, Coach," she said. "Give 'em hell, Sanderson," she said, nodding to the man she had knocked out of starting position.

"Thanks for wearing them out," he said, grinning, happy that Coach had left enough time in the game that if they won tonight, he'd be credited with the win.

# Chapter 8: Then

*Summertime, late morning*

Kyle approached the three boys playing catch at the school ball field. "Hey, guys! Do you want to play a pick-up game? We have two bats."

"Wood or aluminum?" the tallest one, a towhead, asked.

"One of each," Loren said, walking up to the group. "Regulation, too."

The towhead looked back at his buddies. They frowned at him. They didn't have to say a word; it was on their faces. 'We don't want to play with a girl.'

"Nah! We're cool just playing catch," he said and turned back to his friends, tossing the baseball underhand.

"I'll tell you what," Kyle said. "If my sister can't hit as far as either one of you, you can have a bat. Just one of them, though."

"And if she does hit further? What then?"

"We play ball," Kyle said, shrugging his shoulder like it was no big deal to lose either a bet or a bat.

The tall one picked up the aluminum bat, hefted its weight, then checked the other. "I'll take this one," he said, taking the wooden bat and setting it on his shoulder. "Go long, guys," he said to his friends, sending them out to center field.

He tossed the ball in the air. *Fwap!*

"Not bad," Kyle said, watching the ball arc high, then drop ten feet behind second base. "Have one of your guys stand where it hit."

"Stay there, Trevor!"

The younger of the two stood where it fell and waited for Loren to hit, grinning at the chance to get a bat for free.

Loren set the aluminum bat on her shoulder, tossed the ball in the air a couple of times, then stopped and kicked at the ground where she was standing.

"What's wrong?" Towhead asked.

"There's a lump here. I'm just leveling it out," she said, smirking.

"You're just stalling," he said. He walked up to her and stood toe-to-toe, looking down at her from his head-taller height. "Why don't you just give me the bat and go home?"

Kyle walked up and stood between Towhead and his sister. "Come on. Step back. Let her swing. We gave you your chance, now let her have hers." Kyle stifled a chuckle. "She's just a girl, after all…"

Loren rolled her eyes. She knew Kyle was aware she could hit stronger and further than he could. Her brother wasn't jealous. It was just the opposite. He was proud of her skill. Plus, these were the jerks who had been terrorizing the special needs kids at the mall the week before. They weren't hurting them physically, but taunting them, making faces at them, mimicking them in a mocking manner, causing at least two of them to cry.

Loren dropped the bat and turned to Kyle, suppressing her smile. "Are you sure we should do this? Won't Dad get pissed if we lose one of the bats on a bet?"

"Don't worry about it," Kyle said. "Worst case, we'll only have one left. Come on. I want to get a quick game in before noon." He looked up at the sun and squinted. "I'd say we have an hour before we have to be home for lunch."

"Okay…" Loren picked up her bat again, kicked at the imaginary lump one more time, then tossed the ball in the air and slammed it.

"Will you look at that," Kyle said as he followed the trajectory. "Even a girl can hit a home run every once in a while."

"I pulled it a little," Loren said, "so it didn't go in the street. Do you want to play a game now? Or do you think you're too good to play with a girl?"

"Ah, shut up. You can keep your old bat. It's cracked anyhow," he said, throwing it down, hoping it *would* crack.

Kyle picked it up and examined it closely. "Nope. Good ash doesn't break easily," he said. "Come on, Loren. Let's go home and eat lunch early. It stinks out here today."

***

"All right, gang," Craig said. "It's almost game time. One more game, and then it's tournament time! The nice thing about that is winning the trophy. We can let everyone keep it at his or her home for a week before we retire it to the school trophy case. Of course, we still have to win it. Everyone ready to play?"

"Yeah! Yeah!"

"Hey, Loren," Kyle said, then nodded to the other team. "Look who we're playing against today."

"Ugh. It's that creepy white-haired kid with the bad attitude." She tiptoed to see better, then stepped away from her companions, verifying what she suspected. "They're all guys on their team."

"That's their problem," Savannah said. "Oh, and hey, look! We have our own cheerleading squad!"

Ms. Roberge was standing beside her van as the cheerleaders climbed out. Some of the group had considered playing on the baseball team at the beginning of the season, but all were classmates of the ballplayers. "Hey, team!" the former assistant coach called out. "We're here to cheer you on!"

"Cool!" and "All right!" comments bantered about the dugout, lifting the mood of the team even higher.

"We're going to have an upside-down game today," Craig said and paused, waiting for their reaction.

"Huh?"

"We'll reverse our normal batting order and shift our playing positions one spot to the right. First base plays second, second plays third, and so on. This game won't count for the tournament. That starts next Tuesday. This is a practice, warm up, whatever you want to call it."

"Upside-down game is cool," Kyle said, then bent over and looked back at the team from between his legs, not quite standing on his head.

"Lookie, lookie!" a voice cried out from the bleachers, then laughed and squealed excitedly.

The Best Team Ever looked at what was now an animated group copying Kyle. They were now dancing, bending over, cheering and laughing. Four special needs kids from school had come to watch the game with their foster parents. Now all six of them — adults and children —were clapping and dancing, inspired by the antics Kyle had started with his mock headstand.

"Me, too!" Savannah said, copying his bent-over pose.

"Me, three!" Loren said, then the whole team presented their backsides to the air and the other team, getting ready for their upside-down game.

"Retards," Whitey said, then turned away.

"Hey, hey, hey," his coach said, his hand on his son's elbow, reining him in and pointing him back to their dugout. "You can't say that in public," he said softly, patting his back gently.

"Yeah, well they are," he huffed.

"José, I want you to pitch today," Craig said. "Loren, you're catching. Everyone else, move to the right. Got it?"

"Yes, Coach!" they called out, assuming their unfamiliar positions. "This is fun!"

The giddiness continued for the team. Their good spirits resulted in a couple of errors, but they also discovered some unknown strengths.

"Why didn't you tell me you could pitch like that, José?" Craig hollered after two batters were up and down, both struck out.

"No one ever asked," he said, tossing the ball in the air and catching it while the next player came up.

"Come on, Whitey!" the other team's coach called out. "Hit it out of the park, son."

Loren, squatted behind her bigoted nemesis in her temporary position as catcher, wanted to say something evil or caustic but bit her tongue.

*Zing! Thunk.*

"Stee-rike one!" the ump called out as Loren caught José's perfect pitch.

"Dumb luck," the tall towhead grumbled.

Loren snorted a laugh, then turned it into a fake cough, and returned the ball.

*Zing! Thunk.*

"Stee-rike two!"

"It was low and to the inside," Whitey argued, but then shut up, knowing arguing with the ump never worked. That was the coach's job.

José wound up to pitch, then looked over his shoulder. Even though he knew the bases were empty so there was no threat of someone stealing a base, he wanted to stretch out the tension before letting his knuckle ball fly.

*Zing!*

Whitey swung at the erratic ball, making a full turn and a half as he spun around, missing contact completely.

*Thunk.* Loren caught the ball but didn't return it.

"Stee-rike three! And you're out. Next team."

"Caught a little air there, did ya?" Loren asked.

"Bitch! You'd better keep your mouth shut!" Whitey said, his face an inch from hers.

"You said what?" she asked, her nose up to his chin, ready for him to back down.

"Ahem!" the umpire vocalized loudly, then shouldered in between the two. "You're out, Whitey. Take the field."

"Two, four, six, eight! Who do we appreciate?" the cheerleaders cried out.

"The Best Team Ever," their parents, friends and family replied.

"Game's not over yet," the other coach huffed. "Come on, team. Get the lead out and catch those fly balls."

"Don't worry about it," Whitey said, then turned to the crowd and hollered. "It's gonna be three up, three down when I'm done with them. Easy outs."

The bases were quickly loaded with three of The Best Team Ever's players getting walked. The harder Whitey tried, the worse his throws. "Let someone else pitch!" someone sang out from the sidelines.

Whitey shook his head at his dad. "I got this, Coach," he said. "I was just getting warmed up."

The misery continued, Whitey either giving up hits, beaning the batters, or walking the batters with his erratic pitches.

Finally, Craig waved his white hand towel in the air, trying to get the other coach's attention. The red-faced man finally walked over to meet him behind home base. "What's your problem?" the coach asked.

"I think we ought to call it," Craig said, looking at the umpire to see if he agreed. "We're up twenty-two points on you. It's not a league, or even a tournament, game. Your guys are tired. Take 'em out for an ice cream and maybe an hour at the arcade. We could all use a break."

"We're just wearin' you down now," the coach said, then flinched.

The umpire had startled him when he put his hand on his shoulder. "Come on, Joe. Let the boys save a little dignity. You don't want them losing by fifty points, do you?"

The coach huffed and growled like a dog who had just managed to steal an empty food bowl. "Pbbt! Whatever," he grumbled.

"Hey, Joe. It's just a game," the umpire said. "We're here to teach the kids good sportsmanlike behavior and skills. In that order. Come on. First round of cones is on me."

"Oh, all right…"

The umpire took off his headgear, wiped his forehead with the back of his forearm, then waved his empty hand in the air. "That's all there is for tonight, folks," he said to the crowd. "Let's give these guys and gals a big hand." He dropped his face mask, then clapped, nodding to spectators to encourage them.

Both teams lined up and slapped hands and repeated the obligatory, "Good game, good game," to each other, the other team barely audible.

"That was fun!" Savannah said. "Can we do the upside-down lineup next time, too?"

"Not next time, but we can switch it up at practices every once in a while," Craig said. "Come on. Gather up the gear. I think we've earned a pizza party, what do you think?"

*Thunk!*

"Yeow! You bitch!"

Craig looked up and saw a crowd had gathered beside first base. A couple of parents were reaching between assorted players from the other team and spectators, all student-aged. "What's going on?" Craig asked, approaching the perimeter of the excitement.

"Loren just decked Whitey," Savannah said, her smile wide. "And he deserved it, too!"

"Wait! What? No one deserves to be hit," Craig said, then wedged between two students to assess the damage.

"She hit me in the nose," Whitey whined, tears streaming down his cheeks and blood streaming through the fingers he held above his mouth.

Loren patted the shoulder of the young girl clutching her. "It's okay," she said, ignoring Whitey, her dad, and the hullabaloo around her. She looked up and saw a concerned and familiar face. "I think your mama's here to take care of you. It's okay. I'll see you at church on Sunday, all right?"

"Uh, huh," the young blonde with Down Syndrome said. "Thank you, Laurie."

Craig huffed, not knowing whether to holler at his daughter for hitting someone — his first reaction — or to wait and get all the details first.

"Sorry, Coach," Loren said, making sure she took the family aspect out of the exchange by the way she addressed him. "I guess I sort of lost it."

"You think? Loren, I'm going to have to ground you from the next game. Maybe two games, depending on the circumstances."

"Are we still on for pizza?" Kyle asked.

Craig took a deep breath. No reason to punish the whole team for something his daughter did. "Yeah, sure. Come on. We'll deal with the negative after the party. Cheese and pepperoni pizzas for everyone!"

***

"Hey," José said.

"Hey," Loren replied.

"Are you going to be okay? I mean, I'm sure you had a good reason for decking him. Shoot, I think we're all jealous 'cause we wanted to do that, too."

"Yeah, well, you all showed restraint." Loren shook her head, then looked up at José and grinned. "You know the worst part about all this?" she asked, her eyes swollen with tears of sadness.

"Nope."

"It's not missing out on a game or two, or even the lecture I know I'm going to get. It's letting my dad down. I hate to disappoint him."

"Yeah, I know what you mean. I feel the same way about my mom. So, what happened?"

"He called me a bitch. Twice. Once when he was at bat, the other time when I went up to Carsy to give her a hug."

"What? You hit him because he cussed at you?" José asked.

"No, not that. That didn't bother me. Much. I didn't hit him because he called me a bad name. But he said, 'Look at the bitch hugging the retard,' or something like that. I was so mad, I don't remember exactly what he said. I just know I was here one moment," Loren indicated a spot to her right side, "and then the next second," she pointed to her left side, "I was pulling my fist away from his face. I don't even remember throwing the punch."

"Well, I'll spare you the lecture," Craig said, having overheard the conversation, "but I'll have to bench you for a game or two. Let's just see how it goes. Make sure you show remorse to the team. And to me. I don't want this to become a habit, either with baseball or anywhere else. I'm just glad his dad was so embarrassed that it was a girl who decked his son that he wasn't going to press charges or make a stink."

"Yeah, well, they're stinky enough," Loren said.

"Two games. You want to try for three? Remember, remorse."

"Yes, Dad," she said, then gave him a hug. "Thanks for skipping the lecture."

# Chapter 9: Now

"I'm sure glad the food court keeps their thermostats low to compensate for all the ovens and grills kicking out extra heat. I need to chill my core before tonight's practice," Loren said, then took an extra big bite of her kraut dog.

"You know, playing baseball all your life, I thought you'd have had your fill of hot dogs," José said, stirring his bowl of Chinese noodles and teriyaki chicken.

"Ah, but they don't offer sauerkraut in the stands. Plus, this is a Polish sausage, not an American wiener."

José looked up. "Looks like we're not the only ones who decided to hang out at the mall. Frankie Johnson is over there checking it out, too," he said, nodding to the team's star hitter who was strutting away from the top of the escalator.

"That arrogant ass...trophysicist!" Loren hissed in rage, then giggled. "Excuse me. I have zero tolerance for egomaniacs. Did you know he started his own fan club?"

"Really? Does he pay his bills by check, hoping the payees will hold onto his autograph rather than cash it?" José asked, laughing.

"No, no," someone called out in fear.

Loren and José both pushed away from their table and stood up quickly, looking for the source of the ruckus.

"Yum, yum," Frankie said, pretending to lick the ice cream cone he had taken from the boy in the wheelchair.

"Give it back!" the preteen yelled, awkwardly slamming his fist down in frustration.

Without saying a word to each other, Loren and José moved in on either side of Frankie, penning him in.

"Give it back to him!" Loren said, her fists clenched at her side.

Frankie looked down his nose at her and snorted. "Well, lookie here. It's the token player, this month's gimmick to bring more butts to the stands and bucks to the club."

"Folks were getting tired of watching you swing and never connecting," José said, moving so close to Frankie that the tall pinch hitter had to step back in order to see him.

"Speak for yourself, you puny wetback."

"Oops!" Loren said, then intentionally bumped into Frankie's hand, shoving the melting ice cream cone he had swiped from the boy into his chest. "I guess that's not a problem, though, since it wasn't your food to begin with."

She turned to the stunned boy in the wheelchair and squatted beside him. "Don't worry, Sweetie. I'll get you another one," she said with a big smile.

Frankie wedged himself between Loren and the now happy youth, nearly knocking her over. "It may not have been my cone, but it *was* my shirt. You owe me another one!" he growled.

"Well, big fella…" she said, standing up. She paused, waiting to continue just to irritate him.

"Yeah?" he growled, his jaw clenched, his elbow pulled back as if he was ready to punch her.

She turned and took two steps away from the boy so he wouldn't hear, forcing Frankie to follow her. She looked up at him and whispered, "I'll let you in on a secret."

He bent close to hear her, his hand now dropped at his side.

"Clothes are washable," she hissed, "especially cotton tee shirts."

"Why you…" he roared, and stood up tall again, elbow back, returning to his punching stance.

"Whatever you do, don't call her a bitch," José warned. "You won't like what happens if you do."

Frankie turned from Loren to José, ready to slug someone. Or something. Anything. "What?" Frankie asked José snidely. "Does that mean you're gonna hit me if I do?"

"Nope. She can take care of herself," José said, and tapped the young man on the shoulder, letting him know that he was moving him and his wheelchair to the next table, keeping him from potential danger. "But from what I understand, you've been in a few 'roid-enhanced fights in the last few months. I don't think you can afford to be benched. Again."

Frankie thumped his chest like a gorilla. "This is all me. Not a drop of steroids in me."

"You keep telling yourself that," José said. He walked up to Loren and put his hand through her elbow, showing their solidarity. "Maybe you'll get one of the 'me, myself, and I' fans in your fan club to believe you're clean."

José remained stone-faced, but Loren and the handicapped boy laughed at Frankie, enraging the tall man even more. "Shut up, bitch! And you, too, Rickie Retardo!" Frankie screamed.

"Is there a problem, Frankie?" Coach Hanover asked, coming over with a cafeteria tray loaded with various food items and drinks. He set the tray down at the table the wheelchair-bound young man was seated at, then assumed his angry-coach-to-umpire stance, standing nose-to-nose with the vain and obnoxious star hitter.

"No. No problem, Coach," Frankie said, then took a step away, inhaling deep then huffing it out. "But you'd better keep these two away from me if you know what I mean."

"No," Hanover replied coolly, "I don't know what you mean. You three are all on the same team. Either get along or get out. You're a free agent, Frankie — working on a game-to-game basis. If you want to play somewhere else, check your contract and make sure you abide by it, giving us plenty of notice before you split. I'm done babysitting you." He sat down in front of the handicapped youth, pulled the food tray toward him, and started to unwrap one of the items.

"No problem," Frankie said in a deep, threatening voice. He turned to the boy in the wheelchair and said, "I wasn't gonna eat your stupid ice cream cone, either. Retard."

Coach Hanover slammed his hands on the table and stood up. "Okay, you're out," he growled. "Don't even bother coming back to the locker room. I'll send your gear to the address of record. There's no room in my club for a jerk like you. We can't afford the bad publicity."

"You can't do that!" Frankie said, his voice squeaking in shock.

"I just did," the coach said coolly. He sat back down across from his nephew and finished unwrapping the paper from the basket of fish and chips. "Are you hungry, bud?" he asked, holding up a French fry.

"Yeah. Thanks, Unc."

\*\*\*

"Hey, Bubba," Frankie said into his cellphone, as he strolled through the parking lot to his cherry-red Maserati. He climbed in and pushed the start button, then cranked up the air conditioner to full blast. "I think we can help each other out. How about meeting me behind our favorite sports bar in an hour? Yeah, that's the one. See ya there."

***

Loren looked down at her watch. "Shoot! I forgot they set me up for a meet and greet at Everyone's Favorite Sports Stuff."

José picked up the bags from the floor beside him, filled with the custom-made tee shirts he had ordered for the Boys and Girls Club. "Well, Bud," he said, standing up. "It was nice meeting you. You have a great uncle. It's a pleasure working for him." José reached out and took the boy's unsteady hand and shook it. "If I see you at tonight's game, I'll hit one for you."

"Out of the park?" Bud asked.

"I'll try."

"Me, too," Loren said, wrapping both of her hands around Bud's other hand. "I mean, if I see you, I'll try to hit one out of the park for you, too."

Bud's hands started waving erratically, excited to have two ball players pay attention to him.

"Thanks for what you did for him earlier," Coach Hanover said softly.

"Shoot — it was nothing. I actually enjoyed it," Loren said. "Although, I think it would have been more fun to bloody Frankie's nose," she added, throwing an air jab.

José sputtered and laughed at the mental imagine, remembering the first time she had hit someone. "What? And take away my fun? I haven't punched anyone…ever!"

"I don't want anyone hitting anyone else," Hanover said. "I just got rid of one player. He may not have been the best, but between injuries and holdouts, I'm running short of good hitters. I don't want to lose you two, too."

"No worries," Loren said. "But I really do have to scoot."

"Which means I do, too," José said. "Remember? I drove."

"Duh! We have to go change clothes first, too."

"We?" José asked.

"Aren't you coming, too? I'm sure you have as many fans as I do. More since I'm the new kid on the mound." Loren grabbed him by the elbow. "Come one, sweetie."

Hanover and José looked at each other. "Sweetie?" they whispered at the same time.

"Don't ask me," José said, looking sideways to avoid direct eye contact with his coach. "It's the first time she's ever called me that."

"We're just friends," Loren said, patting the coach on the shoulder.

"He's not interested in me that way. Thank God!"

Coach Hanover suppressed a smirk, wiping under his nose to cover any residual traces. "Come on, Bud. Your mom will clobber me if we don't get back in time. I promised her I'd only take you out for two hours."

"B…b…but ice cream?" Bud whimpered.

"I'll get you one the next time," Loren said. "I promise. See you tonight!"

As they passed through the giant glass doors of the mall, José said, "Beat you to the car."

"Yeah, probably," Loren said, "Since I can't remember where you parked and I don't want to get sweaty."

"Yet," they both said at the same time.

Loren looked at him and laughed at the coincidence. "I don't know about you, José. We just met, but it seems like we've known each other for years."

José felt a blush rising so looked away. "It's because we both love the same thing: baseball."

The two rode in silence toward the stadium, then Loren spoke up. "Hey, I think we might be able to get away without being in uniform. If you pull up in front of the club office, I'll run in and get the box of giveaways. You won't even have to park."

"Good idea. The car will stay cooler, too."

"Like I said, we both like the same things," she said.

"And think the same way," he finished.

She got out of his Camaro and said to herself, "Yeah. Too bad you're gay."

As soon as she shut the door, José huffed and said, "Yeah, too bad you think I'm gay."

A fast two minutes later, Loren was back with the ice chest packed with candy bars, stickers, and mini pennants. José, deep in thought, didn't see her approach. She slapped the top of the car twice. "Wake up, slow poke."

José shook his head, trying to erase his frustration at the dilemma he had caused by letting her think he was someone he wasn't, then pushed the button, releasing the trunk lid. "Do you need a hand?" he offered, even though he knew she didn't.

"Nope, I got this. Hey, before we go, can you get out for a minute?"

"Sure," he said. He got out and stood next to his car. "What's up?"

"How do I look?" she asked, and turned around slowly, pulling the wrinkles out of her snug tank top.

"Looks good to me. I mean, you don't have any mustard stains, if that's what you meant."

"Yes, sweetie," she said. "That's what I meant. I don't need a fashion evaluation, even though I'm sure you have better taste than I do when it comes to clothes. As far as I'm concerned, if it feels good — and covers all the modesty sites — it's good for me."

"Why would I have better taste in clothes?" he asked.

"Well, because, you know…" she said, suddenly embarrassed at being called out on a subtle preconceived prejudice that gay men were better dressers. "Come on. I don't want to be late," she said to change the subject, then hopped in the car.

"Right…" José said, then got in and buckled up. "Hispanic guys have good taste, right?"

Loren laughed nervously. "Yeah, that's what I meant."

José resisted the urge to pat her on the thigh, to tell her that no matter what his age, ethnicity or sexual orientation, she was his friend, and he wasn't going to jump her bones or disrespect her. Hopefully, she'd come to that conclusion on her own. Better sooner than later, though. They would, most likely, be together on the same team for at least one season, getting to know each other better. Then again, as great a pitcher as she was, she might get picked up by the majors before the end of the month.

"We're here, sweetie," José said.

"Sweetie?"

"Hey, if you can call me that, then I can, too. What's good for the goose is good for the gander and all that, right?"

"Yes, sweetie," she said, then punched him in the upper arm gently. "Pop the trunk, would you?"

"I'll get it. You lead, I'll follow. You're the one who was invited. I'm just your backup."

"Thanks! I'll just run into the ladies' room first and fix my ponytail. Dang strays."

José ran his fingers through the front of his hair, bringing a thick coal-black shock of waves off his forehead. He then flipped his head back dramatically and closed his eyes. "Yeah, I know what you mean. I have all this hair and can't do a thing with it," he said with a laugh, then opened his eyes. "Uh, oh. Looks like we might have company. Look." He nodded to the red Maserati with plates 'GR8H1TR'parked in the handicapped spot — no handicapped plate or hangtag visible.

"Frankie the Screwup," she huffed. "Oh, well. He's probably going somewhere else. At least, I hope he is."

"That's two of us. Go ahead and get spruced up. I know the drill."

"Thanks, José. I owe you one."

***

No one he knew was in the store yet, other than the assistant manager who had a crush on him. "Hey, Andrew!" José said, dropping the goodie-laden cooler at his feet to shake the slim built young blonde's hand.

"My favorite player," Andrew gushed. "I thought only Loren was coming today. She's good, I'm sure, but when are they gonna let you start? You're the fastest around!"

"I think they're making use of my fielding skills. I'm sure when the time comes, I'll be back on the mound."

"I'd let you on my mound any day," Andrew whispered, then giggled. "I'm sorry. That was wrong. Come on. I have a table set up in the back."

Loren met the two men and helped them straighten out the tablecloth and placards. "You'd better go do a mirror check," she said to José. She pulled her comb out of her back pocket. "You have a few strays, too."

"I think they look sexy," Andrew said, smiling.

"Gotta look my best for the photos," José said, accepting the comb. "I'll be right back."

José spotted a Sammy Sosa bobblehead doll on the way back to the restrooms. He picked it up to see if it was in the same collectible series he had, then heard him.

"Not here, you idiot. I said to meet out back. I don't care how hot it is," Frankie growled.

"Give me a sec. I gotta take a piss. I'll be there when I'm good and ready. And don't ever call me an idiot."

Bubba's angry voice was hard to mistake; Frankie's even more discernable. Nothing good could come out of those two meeting in a back alley.

José stepped away, out of view of the restrooms. When he heard Frankie's heavy footfalls down the hall, heading toward the rear exit, he put the bobblehead back and followed.

Before the door shut, José grabbed a pair of team embroidered sports socks from a sales bin. He tossed them onto the threshold to keep the automatic door from sealing shut, then stepped into the stockroom and eavesdropped.

"We gotta do something about Hanover," Frankie said, his voice raised in anger.

"Not so loud," Bubba said. "And I've been saying that for ages. We can't do it without some real damning evidence, though. My dad thinks that guy breathes and shits baseball."

"Well, how about we get rid of your old man instead? When you're the owner, you can fire Hanover whenever you want. You do have a copy of the will naming you as sole heir, right?"

Bubba's eyes widened, shocked that anyone would suggest that he kill his own father. Then he remembered the warning from Paco. If he didn't sign over the team to him, he'd spend the next two weeks being carved into earrings and lampshades. He shuddered at the thought of

Paco's tool kit. Whether it was human remains clinging to the saws and knives, or deer or elk, it didn't make a difference. There was no place on earth he could hide from the De Luca family if he didn't pay up.

"What's the plan, Frankie? And it better be good."

# Chapter 10: Then

*End of baseball season*
*For The Best Team Ever*

"Hey, Mama. Why don't we invite the Forrests over for dinner? They've done so much for me, letting me spend Friday nights over there, not to mention all the hours Coach spends with the team. You said you don't have to work tomorrow night and I know they love Mexican food." José laughed and added, "They thought the enchiladas at El Charro were the best, but they've never had yours."

Elena gave a weak smile. She didn't know how to tell him they would be leaving in two days. The boss at her second job said a man named Luis De Luca had called and asked if she still worked there. He lied for her, telling him she had never worked there, but it was too close. If José's uncle had found her, his brother — José's biological father and notorious drug dealer — would be close behind. Too close.

"Tomorrow night?" she asked. "Yes, tomorrow night will be fine. I'll go to the market in the morning. You ask them to come when you're at your party tonight."

"Aren't you coming, too? You're invited. I think Coach Forrest likes you," José said, then chuckled. "I like him, too. He'd be a good dad, but I don't know if I'd want a sister."

"Why not? Loren's a nice girl."

"I know. I'd rather have her as a girlfriend, though."

"Oh, my little boy is growing up to be a man. You're having urges, yes? Oh, you better not act on them. I don't know about boys," she babbled. "Maybe I should talk to Craig and ask him…"

"Mama! No! Do not ask him about me or how to raise a son. You're doing fine. I haven't been in any trouble, right?"

"*Sí.* You are a good boy. Yes, I can go to the fiesta tonight, but I will be late. I have to take care of something first."

"Mama," José asked softly, "Are we moving again?"

"*Sí.* You are so smart. We have to leave again. I'm so sorry. You will make friends in the next town, I'm sure. Please, don't let it bother you for tonight. Forget that you know…"

"Yes, Mama," José said dejectedly. "I'll make sure I return the glove I borrowed from Loren tonight. And anything else."

*\*\*\**

"All right, all right," Craig said, clinking his fork on the side of the pitcher of soda to get his team's attention. "Settle down, everyone. I have some awards to hand out." He shuffled through the file folder of certificates he had printed out at work. "All right. First, how about 'The Most Improved Player?'"

"Yeah, how about it?" Sammy called out. "And how do we know someone didn't cheat on totaling the ballots?"

"Well, Sammy," Craig said, "Sometimes you just have to trust other people."

"Yeah, those who don't trust can't be trusted," Savannah hollered. "At least, that's what my mom says."

Sammy blushed as everyone laughed at him. "Okay, okay. I'll trust you, Coach. Sorry to interrupt." He paused, then lowered his head and said, "Not," so only Ray Ray and Sheldon could hear him.

"Most Improved Player award goes to Savannah Smithson! Congratulations, Savannah. We look forward to having you on next year's team, too." Craig handed her the certificate, then shook her hand and gave her a high five.

Boos and yays followed the announcements of all the other winners: Best First Baseman, Outfielder, Team Spirit. What everyone was waiting for, though, were the two most coveted awards: Best Hitter and Fastest Pitcher.

"Now," Craig said, "the winners of these first certificates were determined by votes from your peers."

"Who?" Ray Ray asked.

"Peers are folks just like you. In this situation, your peers would be your fellow players. However, the best hitter and fastest pitcher awards were determined by hard, cold facts. Your RBI, that is 'runs batted in' for those of you who don't know…"

Everyone laughed, including Elena who had just come in, trying to be unobtrusive by sitting at the back and not joining the group at the long table.

"Come on in and join us, Elena," Craig said, smiling widely at her surprise appearance. "We're just handing out certificates, but we still have plenty of pizza and root beer left. Help yourself."

"Thank you, thank you," she said, then pulled a chair over to sit next to her son.

Craig continued. "I think some of you noticed that we had a radar gun at a few of the games this season. Our friend, Officer O'Neal, offered to be in charge of the stats for pitching. We only had use of it for two games, though, so only five pitchers were rated."

"So, who is the fastest pitcher and the best hitter?" Sammy called out. "And what do they win?"

Craig waved the certificates in the air. "They win a homemade, desktop published certificate and bragging rights for the rest of the season. Oh, wait! It's the end of the season. All right, how about bragging rights until we start up next year. I'm hoping all of you will still be around."

José looked at his mother as she looked at him. Both of them grimaced. "It's okay, Mama," he said. "I'll make new friends."

She patted him on the shoulder, then turned her attention to the finest man she had ever known and her secret lunch date for the last four weeks, Craig Forrest.

"And the best hitter is…Loren Forrest! Come on up here, Loren."

"Boo! Hiss!" Sammy, Ray Ray, and Sheldon called out.

"Maybe I should make another certificate," Craig said, glaring at the trio. "How about worst sportsmen?"

"We're just messin' with you, Loren," Sammy said. "You know that, right?" he asked, then bent his head and coughed the word, "Not."

"Yeah, yeah, just messin' with you," Ray Ray and Sheldon agreed, then mimicked the coughed word.

They weren't fooling anyone, but Craig still had another award. Plus, he didn't want to sour Loren's award by disrupting it with the scolding of the three whiners.

"And, according to the City of Gilbert Arizona's second radar gun, the fastest pitcher in The Best Team Ever is…"

"Come on, Coach," Kyle called out. "Spit it out!"

"The fastest pitcher for the Best Team Ever is Loren Forrest! Way to go, darlin'!"

Loren stood up and bowed to each area of the gathering, taking off her hat in mock chivalry, then rushed her dad, giving him a linebacker hug that almost knocked him off his feet. "Thank you, thank you, thank you. I owe it all to genetics and the best coach ever: my dad. Thanks, Dad, for spending all your spare time for us, and even taking time off work. I think I speak for everyone when I say, you really are the best coach ever. Yesterday. Today. Tomorrow. Probably forever!" Loren started clapping, and then everyone in their section of the pizza parlor did, too.

Salvador, the restaurant's owner, came up and applauded beside Craig. "Thanks for letting us be your team's hangout," he said. "And next year, we will sponsor you! Your tee shirts with iron-on decals are cute, but we'll get real professional jerseys next year. Here! Here!"

"And there's nothing greater that I can add to that," Craig said. "Thanks, Salvador. Everyone, if your parents are here and you're ready to go home, I'll see you next season or around town or whatever. Otherwise," he looked down at his watch, "I'll be here for another half hour or so if you need a ride home."

"Congratulations, Loren," José said, coming up to shake her hand.

"It was close," Craig said. "She beat you by that much," he said, holding his thumb and finger a scant half-inch apart. "Either way, sixty-one or sixty-one and a half miles per hour is pretty danged fast."

"I guess I'll have to practice more," José said. "Oh, by the way," he said, turning to Craig. "My mama and I would like to invite you and your family to dinner tomorrow night. She's making chicken enchiladas."

"Oh, we'd love to come. What time?"

"Six o'clock," Elena said. "Unless that's too early. They can stay in the oven if you can't make it…"

"Six o'clock is fine," Craig said, his eyes bright as they connected with hers. "We'll have to find another way to keep in touch since baseball season is over," he added.

Elena blushed, then tipped her head down and looked sideways at José. They both took a deep breath, but it was José who looked up and answered. "I don't think we'll stay here too long. We have to move."

"*Have* to? Is there something I can do?"

Elena's head shook back and forth as she bit her bottom lip. That creep who had got her pregnant when she was only sixteen had ruined her life. Not with giving her a child, but with obsessively chasing her from town to town, all over Mexico and the United States, keeping her from finding a husband for herself and a real father for José. "Let's have a good time tomorrow night, okay? Maybe we come back again sometime."

Craig, Kyle, and Loren looked at each other, all of them sad to be losing the two people who had become so close. "Okay. We'll see you tomorrow night at six. Do I need to bring anything?"

"*Sí,*" Elena said and smiled at the prospect of seeing him again. "Your appetites."

***

*Knock! Knock!*

Craig waited a minute, then knocked again.

"Maybe the fan is on in the kitchen and they can't hear us," Kyle said.

"Yeah, go ahead and open the door and holler. They won't mind," Loren said.

*Knock! Knock! Knock!*

Finally, Craig turned the knob. It was unlocked. He cracked the door open, stuck his head in and called out, "Hello. We're here. Anyone home?"

No answer.

"Something's wrong, Dad," Kyle said. "I smell something burning."

Craig pushed the door open further, then he too smelled smoke, too. "José! Elena! Are you here?"

Loren ran into the kitchen, opened the oven door, and smoke roiled out. She quickly shut it and switched on the exhaust fan. "I think the dinner burning is the only fire," she said. "Maybe they went to the store and forgot…"

"I don't think so," Craig said. "Looks to me like they had to leave in a hurry." He handed Loren the bright yellow gift bag with her name on it. "I guess this is for you."

Loren reached inside and pulled out the paper towel and rubber band-wrapped ball glove. "'Thanks for the loan,' it says." She opened up the glove and saw another smaller package. She took off the reclaimed gift paper wrapping. "Ahh. It's rose cologne," she said. "How sweet."

Unexpected tears fell as she realized he was gone for good. "I hope they're okay," she said.

Craig came up and put his arm around his daughter's shoulder. "Elena told me that they had to move around a lot because of some bad men. One of them was his José's father. He was a murderer and did a lot of other bad things, too. She didn't want her child to grow up around him and his brothers and all the drugs and crime. She's been on the run with José ever since he was born."

"They're gonna be hard to find," Kyle said, feeling uncomfortable in the abandoned home.

"You're right there. All we can do is pray and hope they're safe. If Elena doesn't want to be found, calling the cops and having them look for them wouldn't be the best idea."

"Yeah, but can *we* look for them?" Loren asked.

Craig shook his head. "Nope. Elena's a clever woman. I'm sure she has it sorted out. I don't know if you noticed, but at the party last night, she had a very big backpack with her, stuffed so full that the top wouldn't zip closed. I'd say she was ready to go then. I didn't see the bag in the bedroom. She's probably set with everything they need."

"But, Dad," Kyle said. "What if the bad guys caught them?"

"If they had caught them, I don't think the bedroom window would be open. I'll bet that's how they got out. Plus, there's no blood anywhere…"

"Da-ad!" Kyle and Loren said.

"Come on, kids. There's nothing to do here. Let's go home and I'll make pancakes for dinner."

# Chapter 11: Now

*Everyone's Favorite Sports Stuff*

"Hey, Loren," José said, coming to sit next to her at the table overflowing with Tempe Tornadoes bling, brochures, and souvenirs. "Keep smiling so no one suspects anything."

Loren pasted on a huge, phony smile. "Is this good?" she asked, then blinked like an oversized carnival ride character, her head tilting from side to side.

"Now folks will think you're stoned. No, I just don't want you to freak out. I overheard someone planning to kill Weinman."

"What?" she screeched, then remembered to keep cool. Or at least look pleasant to the fans who were queuing up to get their fan memorabilia signed.

Andrew came over from behind the counter, waving his hands above his head to get the store's patrons' attention as he threaded his way through the throng. "Let's give them a few more minutes," he said to the group. "They're still setting up," he turned around and winked at José. "Aren't you?"

José shuffled a few of the pennants around, taking some out of the cup to lay flat on the table. "Just give us a few minutes, folks. We're not going anywhere."

Loren leaned close to José and turned so only he could see her face. "Kill Weinman? You mean Bubba?"

"Yes and no."

"Huh?"

José shook his head, still unable to comprehend the magnitude of what he had just overheard.

"José. Wake up. Tell me what's going on. I'm a big girl. I can handle it. I hope."

Almost close enough to kiss her but resisting the urge, José whispered, "I overheard Frankie and Bubba planning to kill Old Man Weinman. Something about not wanting the sale of the team to go through. Sounds like Frankie has an axe to grind with Coach — probably because he kicked him off the team today. Bubba and Frankie both want him gone, but Old Man Weinman thinks the sun rises and sets on Hanover. But the big motivation is that Bubba has to come up with some mighty big bucks — probably a gambling debt — in a hurry. If the old man dies now and he's the heir, he'll get the team. That way, he can make Frankie happy by canning Coach, plus he'll be able to sell the team or trade it to cancel his debt or whatever. But Bubba has to be the one to inherit it. Word on the street is the old man who disinherited him until he could prove himself an asset to the team as a coach. His lackluster performance as even an assistant coach has everyone talking."

"But…but…"

"Yeah, heavy, huh?"

Andrew weaved his way to the back of the table and placed a hand on José's shoulder, startling him. "It's all right," Andrew said. "I don't bite. Hard," he whispered, then stood up and addressed both of the ball players. "Ready?" he asked.

"Go for it," Loren said, winking at José as she squeezed his knee under the table.

"All right, everyone," Andrew said, addressing the two dozen fans. "Let me introduce you to two of the greatest players ever to grace the field here in beautiful downtown Tempe: Loren Forrest and José Bosque!"

The two players stood up and waved. "She's much better looking up close, right?" José declared to the group, patting her on the back.

"Yeah! Yeah!"

"And you are, too," a woman in the rear of the group said. "How much to buy you?"

"Sorry, ma'am. I'm not for sale. At least, not yet. I'm still under contract unless the majors call me up."

The whole crowd laughed. "And only my baseball skills are for sale," José added.

"Darn," Andrew whispered, then went back to the checkout counter and cash register.

Loren and José busied themselves signing brochures, pennants and chocolate bar wrappers, answering questions from their true-blue fans about how they liked Tempe and the Tornadoes. "How much for a photo?" one person in the crowd asked.

"No charge," José said. "But if you happen to make a donation to the Boys and Girls Club in your town, I'm sure the kids and parents will appreciate it."

"Wow! You're good," Loren whispered.

José wanted to say, "I'd love to show you," but only managed a weak grimace.

"Are you all right?" she asked when the crowd had thinned out.

"Not really. I took a minute to call the anonymous tip line and told them what I overheard. Yeah, right. Anonymous. Caller ID will let them track me wherever I am. Still, I had to do something."

"Do you think we ought to call Coach and let him know his life is in danger?"

"It's not Coach they're after; it's Albert Weinman. He's got bodyguards already, so he should be safe."

"Yes," Loren said, picking up the pencils and pennants and putting them back in the boxes, "But Bubba knows his father's routine and the guards aren't going to be suspicious of the old man's son."

"Then we'll just have to trust that the cops will take care of it. Come on, we have a game in a few hours. I'll drop you off at your place, then I'm taking a nap."

"Really? You can do that before a game?"

"No, but it sounds better than saying I'm going home to pace the floor and bite my fingernails."

Loren punched him playfully in the upper arm. "I'm so glad I have you around. I don't know how I'd manage being on this team without you."

"You'd do fine, I'm sure. Thanks for helping *me* out."

"Anytime, sweetie," she said. She stood up and handed him the leftover pennants. "For the Boys and Girls Club?"

"Sure. Thanks. Now, let's get out of here."

\*\*\*

"Don't you just hate it when your family makes a big deal out of you being on the team?" Felipe said.

"Nope," all the players within hearing distance agreed.

"I mean…"

"Felipe, your dad is your biggest fan. I swear, I can hear him screaming for you when you come up to bat," José said.

"Yeah, well," Felipe said, his face reddening with embarrassment that he had even brought the subject up.

"Yeah, at least he comes to every game. My dad still hasn't seen me pitch in the minors," Loren said.

"Yeah, where is he?" José asked, then decided he'd better play dumb. "And your mom? Doesn't she like baseball, too?"

"Don't have one," Loren said coolly, then bent to re-tie her shoe.

"Me, neither," Felipe said. "I guess it's better to have one great parent than two deadbeats. I mean, I really am proud that my dad gets so excited. It's just kind of embarrassing sometimes. What about you, José?"

"I'm cool with what I have. One deadbeat out of the picture and a mom who's the greatest but can't travel."

"Oh, that's too bad," Loren said. "I hope she can watch the games on cable."

"Yeah, she does," José said. "Enough of this mushy stuff. We have a game to win!"

*Oooh! Barracuda!*

"Your phone is ringing, Loren," José said, then stepped away so she could get to her locker.

"Hello? Oh, hi, Dad! You will? And Kyle's coming, too? How'd you swing that? No worries. At least I got through the first game jitters. All right. Come down to the locker room after the game. I'll let them know you're coming. Love ya! Bye!" Loren set her phone on silent and put it back in her locker. "My family's going to be here tonight! Woo hoo!" she crowed, then mumbled, "Oh, no," and covered her mouth and quickly sat down on the bench.

"First night jitters all over again?" José asked.

"Uh-huh."

"Take a deep breath. There's always going to be a first night or first day for everything. You're a big girl. You've survived more intense situations, I'm sure," José said, his hand gentle on her shoulder. "Just take a deep breath and visualize yourself tomorrow morning, eating pancakes with Coach and Kyle, talking about your second win."

Loren looked up at José and squinted. "How do you know about the morning after pancake breakfasts? And how did you know my dad was Coach?"

José choked on his drink, then set it down. "Doesn't everyone have pancakes?" he asked innocently. "And I'm pretty sure I heard somewhere that your dad has coached you since you were yay high," holding his hand down by his knee.

"All right, all right," Coach Hanover said, coming in with his clipboard. "Gather 'round and hear the lineup. We're looking good, but we're still three games out of first place. What are you going to do about it?"

"Win!" everyone chorused.

"That's my team. Now, I have some news to share with you this afternoon. Some might say sad news, but whether it's good, bad or sad, it's still news. First, I had to let Frankie go this afternoon." The coach waited for the expected groans and chuckles to die down, then began again. "I want to remind you that your presence in the community has to be perfect. You are a reflection on the club. That means no public intoxication, fights, or inappropriate behavior of any kind. It's in your contract, so please, behave yourselves. I don't want to lose any more players."

"Yes, Coach," the team said.

"Now, the second news. I guess it's actually more important, but if I had told you about it first, you wouldn't have listened to me give you your Civics and Civility 101 lesson." The coach waited for the second round of chatter to die down, looking over his clipboard as he waited rather than raise his voice.

"Well, are you going to tell us or not?" someone asked.

He glanced over the group, suddenly silent when they saw his mood was even more somber than speaking about getting rid of Frankie. "The team has been sold," he said with an even, unemotional tone.

"Wait! What? To who? Why?" A dozen different simple questions were thrown out at the same time, each one on top of the other. Coach looked down at his clipboard again and licked his lips, waiting once again.

It worked. They stopped talking and waited for the answer.

"I don't know the man's name. Yes, it's a man, although from what I understand, he's the owner of a rather large business and wants the team's new name to reflect that business."

"Don't tell me we're gonna be the Tempe Toilet Bowl Cleansers!" someone hollered. "Or Valley of the Sun Suppositories!"

Another round of wild suppositions and comments erupted, but this time, Coach raised his hand and they silenced immediately. "Don't know whether or not everyone is staying. If your contract takes a sale into consideration, you're safe. If you're a free agent... Well, let's just wait and find out who the buyer is, whether he wants a new coaching staff or not, and if he's happy with all of you."

"Excuse me." A lanky man in a high dollar silk suit wedged his way into the crowded room, his manicured hand loaded with gold and diamond rings waving in the air to get Coach's attention. "Excuse me," he repeated.

"Sir, I'm sorry. You'll have to leave. This is for team members only," the coach said.

"Well, since I just bought the Tornadoes this afternoon, I guess that makes me one of the team, right?" he said, his oversized handlebar mustache almost hiding his broad, toothy grin.

As if a wand had been waved over the stunned gathering, everyone took two steps back, giving the new owner room to speak.

"Good afternoon, team," he said, nodding to acknowledge the members. "Felipe, Sanders, Gonzales," he said, announcing their names one by one with confidence, as if he was calling out the players on his limited-edition baseball cards.

His mustache twitched and his smile faded momentarily when he got to José and Loren. "I see some faces familiar to me from watching you play the last few games, and I also see a couple from when I was playing Little League."

"Hey, Sammy," José said, lifting his chin to acknowledge him. "You forgot to introduce yourself."

Sammy's grin broadened, his dimples stretching into long thin lines. He cut his eyes over to Loren. She was clueless about who he was. "Just call me Sammy, for now," he said, the twinkle remaining as he gave a quick wink to José. "We'll get to know each other more after the game. Correction. After you *win* the game. Go out there and give 'em hell, team!"

"Yeah! Give Yuma hell!" Coach Hanover said, his fist punching the air.

"All right!" "Hell ya!" and "Hoo! Hoo!" calls reverberated through the locker room.

"Take your last-minute leak, chew, or spit because I need to have a quick word with José," Coach said, "and then we'll hit the field."

José followed him into his office. "What's going on, Coach?" he asked innocently.

"I think you know, José. I got a call from the police department this afternoon. Sounds like someone — who shall remain nameless — has a grudge against me and Old Man Weinman. There's extra security hanging around. I just wanted you to know that he or they might be after you and Loren, too."

"You mean, Frankie's pissed because he's off the team…" José said, letting a sly smirk show.

The coach smacked him on the upper arm. "I always knew you were a smart one. Watch yourself and Loren. Not that I think anyone would hurt a woman, but then again, she's a ball player first."

"Yes, Coach. She's already aware of what's going on. She's watching out for me, too."

"That's good to hear. Now let's play ball!"

As soon as he left the locker room, Coach realized that José knew who the new owner was but hadn't shared the information with anyone nor had the new owner called him out by name. "That kid. If I ever had a secret, he's the only one I'd tell."

***

"The seats are over here, Kyle," Craig said. "Front and center, just how I like it. Right behind home plate."

"Shouldn't family of players get box seats?"

"Funny, Kyle. Our business isn't doing that good. Yet. I can't tell you how much it means to me to have you help in the store. I always wished that I could clone myself and be in two places at the same time, but shoot! This is better. You're smarter than I am and more organized."

"Nah, I'm just not all worn out from raising two kids by myself. Watch out, though. Someday, I'll have a family of my own, and then I'll slow down, too."

"By then, we should be able to hire more whippersnappers to fill in. I hope. Until then, let's enjoy the home games," Craig said, then nudged his shoulder against his son's. "What I'd like to do is buy a camper and follow Loren around the country, watching her play wherever she goes."

"Yeah, well that's a great dream. I think one of us had better win the lottery first, though."

"Or fix up our old camper," Craig said. "It may be older than you, but it still has a lot of life left in it."

An attractive woman in her forties double-checked the seat number on her ticket as she waited for them to finish talking. "Excuse me," she said to Kyle. "That's my seat over there."

Kyle turned sideways to allow her to pass. "Dad, coming through."

Craig looked up and blanched. "Elena? What are you doing here?"

Elena's face blossomed into a dimpled smile, her eyes brilliant with joy. "Craig!" she squealed, then stumbled across Kyle to get to her long-lost secret lover.

Kyle awkwardly scooted away from the giggling couple as they moved into each other's embrace. That's more than a friendly hug, he thought as he stood in the aisle, stunned, watching them hold each other tight, as if they'd fall apart if they let loose.

Craig took one more look into her face, and then bent down and kissed her on the forehead. "Oh, how I missed you," he said softly.

Elena tipped her head up, looked him in the eye, then winked. "Your aim is off," she said, then puckered up.

Craig glanced at Kyle and smirked with embarrassment at being so demonstrative in public. Then he remembered that they were all adults now and leaned in and kissed Elena without abandon. He paused, pulled back and looked at her again. He repeated, "Oh, how I missed you."

The giddy woman reached up and wrapped her arms around his neck, grasping her elbows to hold on tight as he stood up straight, clutching her close. "I'm never going to let you out of my sight again!" he declared loud enough that people in the next three rows turned around and looked at him.

Her arms relaxed and settled on his shoulders as she slipped back to standing on her own two feet. "It was a matter of life or death," she said simply, shrugging and grimacing with the admission.

"I should give you the dickens and tell you that you could have come to me or the cops for help, but it doesn't matter," Craig said. "That's all in the past and we can't change it. Please, though, don't do that again. I missed you." He looked up at Kyle and smiled, seeing that he was happy now and over his initial shock. "*We* missed you," Craig clarified. "Loren, too. Did you know she's playing here tonight? Of course, you do. That's why you're here."

Elena giggled. "Loren's playing tonight? Oh, that's right. No, I came to watch José."

"José's playing? So, he's on the Yuma team?" Craig asked.

"No," Elena said, slowly shaking her head. "He's shortstop for the Tempe Tornadoes! He made it to a real ball team. I think he's going to be in the majors soon."

Kyle and Craig looked at each other, then Kyle took the rolled-up game program out of his back pocket. He thumbed through the pages until he found the team roster. "Well, lookie there," he said, pointing to José's picture, then handed the program to his dad. "Looks like he changed his last name. I've seen him play, but I didn't know that he was my old buddy, José."

"*Sí,* he's changed. He keeps the beard, too, just so he isn't too pretty."

Kyle coughed into the side of his fist, then looked up at his father and former best friend's mother, still holding onto each other. "Elena, you never call a man pretty. Handsome, yes. Pretty…not a good idea."

"Wait!" Craig said, then stepped back. "Does Loren know who he is? No, she can't or she would have said something to me. Did she say anything to you, Kyle?"

"Nope, but she did say she had a new friend." Kyle cleared his throat and blushed. "She said she's made a lot of friends, but her best friend is a gay guy, José Bosque."

Elena laughed out loud. "He's not gay. I know he's not. He likes girls. Those other boys on the team, though…" She shook her head and frowned. "They like girls *too* much. But they don't respect them. They bring them up to the room and have parties with them and, no. José said he doesn't want any part of that. When they called him gay, he didn't protest because he said it was easier than explaining."

"So, Loren's best friend is my old buddy José," Kyle mused, then laughed. "Well, at least she has good taste. But boy, is she gonna be surprised. I'll bet he's not just hanging out with her to be friends. Guys don't do that, do they?" he asked, then winked at his dad, still holding onto Elena.

"Not so much. Yes, she'll be surprised. Dollars to donuts, though, José knows who she is."

Elena giggled. "*Sí,* he does. But he said I shouldn't tell anyone. He doesn't know I'm here tonight, though. I have some big news for him." She squeezed Craig tight around the waist. "And now I have two big *newses*! The other one is Craig and I are together again and we don't have to keep it a secret anymore!"

***

"Is it all set up?" Bubba asked.

"Yeah," Frankie grunted. "My guy switched places with the runner in the skybox. He'll slip the old man a cocktail that'll give him one last whoopie, and then you'll own the show."

Paco had slipped into the utility room unnoticed to listen in on the two screw ups. He shook his head, amazed at how inept they were in their plan. "Hey, Bubba," he whispered from three feet away.

Bubba jumped, startled by the nearness of someone in the room after he had just made certain it was empty "Paco?" he asked, blinking rapidly in fear as he stepped backwards, coming up against the concrete wall of the stadium.

"You can save your poison or drug or whatever it was you were going to use to take out Daddy. He already sold the team."

"Huh?" Bubba squeaked.

Paco took a step forward and suddenly had a steely grip on Bubba's throat. "I knew you were bluffing from the start. You were never going to inherit the team. You're a loser six ways over, at least. I'm surprised your daddy hasn't put a contract out on *you*." Paco turned and spat over his shoulder, then released his grip. "You're an embarrassment to everyone who's ever met you. Why don't you take a fast drive over a steep cliff?"

Bubba's eyes cut over to Frankie, but his partner in crime was looking anywhere and everywhere but at the disputing duo. "Frankie?" he whined.

"Hey, it was all your idea, not mine. I just wanted Coach gone." Frankie turned to Paco. "Nice almost meeting you, sir. I'll just leave you two alone," he said, and slipped out the door, sprinting toward the incoming crowd, arms practically swimming through the fans headed towards their seats.

"Looks like it's just you and me, Ass. Coach," Paco said, grinning.

\*\*\*

Loren opened her locker to get her glove but found a package wrapped in paper toweling in its place. "What the…?" She lifted the box up, verifying that her own glove was nowhere to be found. Curiosity rather than anger at the missing equipment had her pulling off the half dozen rubber bands that secured the absorbent paper packaging. She sniffed the reclaimed shoe box, verifying her suspicion. It had to be a new glove. Her father must have noticed her shopping online, putting the mitt in her cart at least five times. She had been leery about investing that much money, so never finished the transactions.

José watched from behind his locker door as Loren pulled the lid off, then squealed in delight at the kangaroo hide glove. She took it out of the box and noticed another paper-towel wrapped parcel held in the palm of the mitt. She hastily unwrapped it and grinned. "Tea rose cologne," she whispered, then opened the bottle and inhaled deeply. She splashed a little on the back of her hand, then swiped it under her neck.

"Hey, look at that!" one of the players said, looking up at the monitor. "Look at them going at it!"

José closed his locker door and looked up at the same time as Loren. "Mom?" he said.

"Dad?" Loren said, then looked over at José as she realized what he had said. "*Your* mom?" she asked.

José looked at her and blushed, gave a slight shrug, then turned back to the monitor as the couple continued their smooch. "Oh, geez…"

"Man, oh man," Felipe said. "Is that your mom," he looked at José, "and your dad," looking at Loren, "making out in the stands?"

Loren's hand dropped down, stunned. She remembered she was holding a bottle of cologne, then brought it back up to her nose and sniffed again. She looked over and asked, "You're José, aren't you?"

"What have you been smoking, Loren?" Felipe asked. "You know it's José."

"Yeah, but you're *José*! My José. I mean…" she stammered as her face went from ash-white, to red, to almost purple.

"I never claimed to be anyone but José," José said.

"But…but…"

Coach Hanover came out and shut off the monitor. "Enough gawking at the Kiss Cam, team. It's game time."

"Here," José said, taking her old glove out of his locker and handing it to her. "I know you didn't get a chance to break in the new glove. We can do it tomorrow. Come on. We can talk about this later. In private," he added, glancing over to the few players who were wondering what the holdup was.

Loren grimaced, then held up her old glove in one hand, the new one in the other. "José got me a new glove," she said, forcing a smile. "I guess I'll have to wait until the next game to break it in, though." She put the new glove back in her locker and looked around, noticing all eyes were on her now. "What are you waiting for? Come on!" she added, adrenaline-fueled excitement overriding her griping gut that was churning in confusion. "Coach says I'm starting tonight and I'm itching for a perfect game."

Cheers and sarcastic jeers flooded the room as the team funneled out of the locker room, down the hallway and toward the stadium. "Are you okay, really okay?" José asked Loren.

"I hope so," she said. "Looks like it's not just my dad and Kyle I have to impress. Your mom's here, too."

José quickly patted her on the back like he would one of the guys. "Ah, don't worry about her. She's seen you pitch before. She's already a fan." *I just hope you don't realize that the team's new owner is your Little League nemesis — the kid who said he was going to have his own team just so he could exclude girls from playing!*

\*\*\*

"Hey, Dad! Here they come," Kyle hollered, keeping his eyes focused forward as his father snuggled and giggled with Elena.

The happy couple stood as a unit, cheering the team as they ran onto the field. "Look at them," Elena said, then waved in the air and whistled. "José! José!" she shouted, trying to get his attention.

José recognized her sharp whistle and searched the area in the stands behind home plate, frowning, hoping that she hadn't risked being discovered by the De Lucas just so she could watch him play. Finally, he spotted her and returned the wave, his automatic smile of love overcoming his fear. Yes, she was with Coach Forrest, side-by-side, practically joined at the hip as Kyle stood five feet away, waving just as wildly.

"You say he didn't know you were coming?" Craig asked when there was a break in the crowd noise. "He looks happy to see you."

"He'll be even happier when he hears the news. You are meeting Loren after the game, right?" she asked.

"That's the plan. You and José will join us, I hope. I mean, we are still family, right?"

"Still?" Kyle asked. "I mean, I wasn't trying to eavesdrop, but…"

"I consider us family," Craig said, then hugged Elena sideways, pulling her closer still. "We just need to make it official. If she'll have me. Us."

"*Sí!*" Elena squealed, her shoulders hunched up in excitement. "Yes, yes, we can make it official as soon as you like. I am a free agent," she added with pride. "No contract."

Kyle snorted a laugh. "Parents," he said and shook his head. "You gotta love 'em."

***

"Psst! Dinner for everyone at the Grandest tonight after the game. New boss is buying," Felipe said to Gonzales. "Pass it down."

"Do we have to go?" Gonzales asked.

Felipe snorted. "If you want to stay with the team, I think it's a good idea, don't you?"

Gonzales's answer was to turn to José and whisper, "Psst! Dinner for everyone at the Grandest tonight after the game. New boss is buying. Pass it down."

José looked up at Coach, caught his eye, then asked, "Dinner at the Grandest tonight?"

Coach stuck his bottom lip out and nodded, then looked away, watching the batter stomp the plate, waiting for the pitch. *Sometimes diplomacy is underrated. Best to play nice from day one than kiss up for the rest of a contract.*

***

Loren pitched two innings before a line drive caught her by surprise, hitting her glove awkwardly, twisting her arm backwards. José ran in from shortstop, caught the ball, and threw the batter out at first. He trotted over to her to give back the ball. "Are you all right?" he asked.

She nodded that she was, but he could see the pain in her face. He

134

looked up and saw the coach asking for a time out. "You might be, but I think that ball hurt Coach more than you."

"Are you all right, Forrest?" Coach Hanover asked.

"Yeah, I'll be fine. It just stings a little."

"Well, finish this inning, and then we'll bring in Lopez. You're doing great," he said, then gave the umpire a thumbs up. "She's fine."

The next two players hit pop ups and were out, giving Loren the break she needed.

"Here," Lopez said when she came to the bench. "Have a snort of this. It'll help."

Loren looked down and saw that the pitcher who was supposed to be her relief was trying to pass her a flask. "No, thanks," she said, then looked away to watch the game.

"What? You too good to drink after me, white girl?" Lopez slurred.

Loren glanced back at him, amazed at his remark, then noticed that others had heard it, too.

"Back off, Lopez," Felipe said through clenched teeth.

José was on deck, choosing his bat, when he felt a chill run up his spine. He looked back and saw Loren surrounded by five players, some sort of altercation erupting. The coach had his back to everyone and was oblivious of what was going on. *Pay attention to the game, José. That's Coach's problem.*

José hit a double on the third pitch, bringing it to two on base. He squinted at the dugout from second base, trying to see what was going on, then gave up. *Focus on the game, José!*

Felipe hit a double, too, and drove in two runs. Two outs came one after the other, then the other team was up to bat.

As soon as Lopez sauntered out of the dugout, glove in hand, grinning at the surprise opportunity to pitch at a home game, Coach smelled the booze on him. "Hold up there, bud. A word."

"Wassup, Coach?" Lopez asked, then hiccupped. "Oops! That one sneaked right out, didn't it?"

"You're drunk and you're benched, Lopez," Coach said, then held his arm out, slowing the exodus of the players. "Hold on, team. We have a change up." He scanned the group, then nodded to José. "You're pitching. Swap gloves."

"He ain't gettin' my glove," Lopez said, shoving his pitcher's mitt under his arm, huddling over it protectively.

"Here," Loren said, offering hers. "It might be small, but your hands aren't that big."

"Wrong handed glove, Little Miss Saltine," Lopez sneered.

"Nah," Loren said, then thumped José on the back as her personal endorsement of his skills. "This guy's good. Very good. Oh, and full of surprises, too. Aren't you, José?"

José chuckled, then swung his left arm around, warming it up. "Been a while, but some things never change," he said, adding a wink.

Loren brought her hand up to cover the blush, then smelled the rose cologne she had put on before the game, recalling the first gift José had ever given her. "Yeah, the more they change, the more they stay the same."

"And look here," the announcer called out to the crowd. "It looks like we have a change in the lineup. Our shortstop — and sometimes second baseman — José Bosque, is pitching tonight."

The stadium chatter rumbled in confusion as folks commented on the highly unusual changeup in player positions.

"Folks, am I seeing things, or is this guy a lefty? I'm pretty sure he plays right-handed when he's in the infield." After a pause, the announcer said, "Yes, folks. Check your brochures. Our own José Bosque fields right-handed and pitches with the left. Now, I don't know about you, but this could get confusing for the hitters. Well, let's hope so! Let's hear it for switch hitters and switch pitchers!"

The crowd roared with cheers, whistles, and air horns, encouraging the players and surprising the stunned team from Yuma.

After phenomenal playing by the Tornadoes and a long string of errors by the Yuma team, Kyle, Craig, and Elena got up to leave at the bottom of the ninth. It looked like another win for the home team. The

Tornadoes were up by eight runs, and with two outs, it looked like it wouldn't be long until the stadium seats were emptied, the fans pouring out, elbowing their way to the exits, the parking lots, and the aftergame parties. The celebrating had already started in the stands with paper cups of lukewarm beer. Bottles of chilled brew were waiting in coolers on pickup truck tailgates and on tap in barrooms, ready for the uninhibited and only partially restrained festivities to begin.

"Where are they?" Elena asked after half an hour had passed and neither José nor Loren had showed up. "Shouldn't they be here by now?"

"Depends on if there's a long line at the showers," Kyle joked, then looked down at his phone. "Oh, shoot. I had my phone off." He pressed the power button and waited. "Yeah. Loren sent me a text. They were asked — and she has that in quotes — to meet the new owner at The Grandest after the game. Anyone else want to go? I mean, it is a public place," he said. "And I promise to keep my shirt on and not dance on the tables."

Elena giggled at his silliness, but both she and Craig knew he only made the remark because he was nervous. New team owners often meant a change in personnel.

"Yeah, I think that's a great idea," Craig said. "Do you want to ride with us?" he asked Elena as they walked out.

"Oh, yes, please. I took the bus here so I didn't have to pay for parking. Not that I have a car…"

"I don't think Dad's going to let you out of his sight again, Elena. Does José know about you two?" Kyle asked.

Elena shook her head and blushed. When they stopped next to the truck, she giggled and said, "Shotgun!" Craig unlocked the passenger door for her. "Same truck?" she asked.

"Now it's the work truck," he said, then whispered, "I'm buying a new one pretty soon. You can help me pick it out. It has to be big enough for a camper."

"A camper?"

"Yeah, so we can follow the team when they play away games," he said and winked.

"Come on, you two," Kyle said as he rearranged hardhats, boxes, and notebooks in the half-sized back seat. "We won't get out of the parking lot until next week if we don't leave now."

\*\*\*

José held onto Loren's elbow as he ushered her into the banquet room. "Wow! They even brought out the fancy china for us tonight," he said as he held out her chair.

"Why didn't you tell me?" she hissed in his ear, then turned around and smiled broadly to the gathering of team members, their families, and the press.

"I did. I told you my name was José," he said and sat down.

"Yes, you said your name was José, but you didn't tell me you were *my* José."

José leaned forward, as if to knock something off his shoe, then spoke so only she could hear. "So, I'm *your* José now?"

"You know what I mean. You tricked me!"

"How could I trick you?"

"You said you were gay!" she whispered harshly, glad that the room was abuzz with voices, canned music, and servers clattering tables, chairs, and service items.

"When?" he mouthed, then looked up at Felipe who was watching the exchange from six feet away.

Felipe laughed out loud when he realized what was happening right before his eyes. "So, she outed you?" he asked, then looked around to be sure no one was listening.

José growled but never said a word.

Felipe laughed again, even louder, then walked over to their table. "You're a smart woman, Loren," he said. "I knew you'd figure it out sooner or later. José's a good guy, though. I should know; he and I have been living together for almost a year now. He's clean, decent, and reliable. I just didn't know until tonight that he went both ways." Felipe chuckled, then tipped back his bottle of beer, chugging it down without pausing. "Both ways in baseball, I mean. The other way, I'm pretty sure he's straight." He tried to take another drink, then realized he had already finished it. "He's straight the other way, too. I mean, we are roommates and I have seen him naked…"

"Felipe!" José and Loren shouted at the same time, both of them equally red-faced.

"Maybe I should leave you two alone. I'm sure you'll get it sorted out. I will tell you one thing, Loren. I'd let my sister date him…and that's saying a lot."

"What's going on here," Sammy said, one arm slung over Felipe's shoulder. "You talking to my surprise of the year? Way to go, José. We'll have to rotate you and Loren for pitching."

"Hey, Sammy," José said. "Your lawyers might want to take a second look at my contract. I had it written in that if the team was sold, whether I go or stay is my choice."

"Oh, José, José, José," Sammy cooed. "Let bygones be bygones. That was years ago. Looks like you're still hanging out with your favorite gal, though. Hey, Loren. Remember me?"

"Uh. No," she said, then looked at José for verification.

"You know," Sammy said, "I've heard about people being almost blind to faces. I mean, they wouldn't even know their own self if they weren't on the other side of the mirror."

"Prosopagnosia," Loren said. "Yeah, I've heard of it."

All three men looked at Loren. "No, I don't think I have it," she said. "I just block out people and memories sometimes. You know, if someone hurt or embarrassed me to the nth degree, I delete them from my emotional database."

"Sounds handy," Sammy said, then reached out to shake her hand.

Loren looked at José and Felipe, wondering what was going on. Both players shrugged, so she returned the gesture and shook his hand.

"Loren Forrest, I'm Sammy Silvestri. I just bought the Tempe Tornadoes. Once upon a time, we played on the same Little League team. I was a jerk. The son of a jerk, too. I used to tease and taunt you, but you were pretty good at getting back at me."

"Real good," José whispered.

"Real good at getting back at me," Sammy said, smiling. "I said I was going to grow up and buy my own ball club and exclude girls from it. Well, I did do the former, but after watching you play throughout college and for the last few weeks here in the minors, I decided there wasn't one good reason on earth that a female shouldn't have the same access to baseball as the guys. Might not be a good idea to play tackle on a pro football team, though. That could be a different story."

"You never met my sister," Felipe said, then mimed a big person with mega muscles.

They all laughed; tension released.

"So, I hope you two stick around," Sammy said.

"Hey, how about me?" Felipe whined comically.

"Get your drinking under control, fast boy, or the only place you're going to play is on the rehab softball team."

Felipe reached out and grabbed a short green bottle of cola from the serving tray on the next table. "Fresh start," he said. "Only dark brown and sugary bubbly for me from now on."

"Hey, there!" Craig called out to José and Loren, Elena on his arm, Kyle at his side. "You didn't think you could skip out on us, did you?"

"Hey, Coach," Sammy said and stuck out his hand. "Long time, no see."

"Sammy? Sammy Silvestri? My God, man. You look just like your mother. Except for the mustache, of course."

"Well, Coach," Sammy said. "You told me a long time ago that I might make a good coach. Seems like running businesses was more in my talent range, so I had to buy a team in order to play coach. Not that I'm going to take over for Hanover," he added, seeing the head coach approaching their table.

"Do you think we can sneak away," José whispered to Loren. "I want to talk to you in private."

"Are you kidding?" she said. "Not a chance. Our parents, coach, friends, team owners… What's so important?"

"I want to apologize."

"For what? Me not recognizing you? Don't worry about it. You still have all the good assets I've looked for in a friend. That hasn't changed," she said.

"Yeah, well, I really want to get out of the friend zone," José said, then rolled his eyes. "If you know what I mean."

"Well, as a matter of fact, I do."

"Great," José said, then put his hand on top of hers.

She moved her hand out from under his. "You mean you want to be my coach or trainer, right?"

José blanched, then took his hand from the table and put it on his lap. "Yeah. Right," he said dismally.

Loren leaned forward, her nose an inch from his so she was cross-eyed. She pulled back to focus. "Not! Nah, you can coach and train me, but not on a professional level."

"Friends?" he asked.

"Don't you know that a guy and a gal who are attracted to each other can't stay in the friend zone for long. Look at those two," Loren nodded to her father and Elena, waiting for the waiter to bring them their drinks. "Mutual attraction seems to run in the family."

"It sure does," he said, smiling at the happy couple.

"José!" Elena squealed, running up to him as he stood up. She snuggled into his chest, then looked up at him. "He's in prison," she whispered. "That sperm donor bastard was arrested and got life in prison. Enrique De Luca will never bother us again. I don't have to run anymore!"

"But Mama," Jose said, his voice low so only she could hear, "You're still an illegal. ICE could get you any time."

"Nope!" she said, then pulled away and stood tall. She gave a 'come hither' look to Craig, and he was at her side in a flash. "I'm getting married soon. Very soon — maybe tomorrow."

"Coach?" José asked, looking up at the man who had meant so much to him years before. "You're going to marry my mother?"

"I'd ask you for your blessing — and I'd be grateful for it — but know that no matter what, I'm going to make your mother Mrs. Craig Forrest. I was without her for the last ten years, and that was eleven years too many."

Loren stood up and approached José and the parents, waiting for them to finish speaking. When there was a lull, she pursed her lips into an exaggerated scowl. "Ew! You'd be my brother," she said to José, then laughed and punched him in the arm. "Sweetie."

José pulled her close, looked up to see who was watching, then decided he didn't care, and kissed her on the top of the head. "Whatever problems we have being on the same team, or even on different teams, we can work through, right?"

"You betcha, Sweetie," Loren said, then reached up and brought his face down to hers. "And you missed."

"It *is* after the game," he said, then kissed her on the mouth, savoring the softness of the lips he'd dreamt about for ages.

"Looks like we're going to have to have some flexibility in players' conduct rules," Coach Hanover said, blushing slightly.

Loren looked back at him. "And shower times," she said and winked.

"And shower times," José echoed, then bent to kiss her again for the second time in what he hoped was an eternity.

***The End***

# A Note from the Author

Thanks for reading TOO FAST FOR YOU, part of THE PLAYERS box set.

If you enjoyed the story, please help others know about what impelled you to finish it by reviewing and recommending it to others.

# Other Books by Dani Haviland

## *ARLIE UNDERCOVER SERIES*

### (romantic suspense based in Alaska and Arizona)

**A Stingray Christmas**: (First book) Anchorage detective on medical leave travels from Alaska to Arizona to see for the first time the son he'd fathered as an anonymous sperm donor. Great and rotten surprises await the cop with the smartest smartphone around.

**The Biggest Heart Ever**: (Book two) When would Arlie learn that trying to do everything by himself could be deadly—and make Charlene a widow before they were married?

**Always a Bigger Fish**: (Book three) Back in Alaska, Arlie finds out he's a target. Will vacationing detective Billy Burke (from THE FAIRIES SAGA) have information to help nab the scalper?

**How to Fix a Broken Life:** (Book four) When Arlie's very pregnant wife is kidnapped by pseudo terrorists, will he be the one to rescue her or will a surprise hero come in to save the day?

**Because You Said So:** (Book five): Can Arlie handle two very pregnant women, an overeager protégé, and a new crook bringing human trafficking to Anchorage and still wear the Santa suit?

## THE FAIRIES SAGA SERIES

## (historical fiction/time travel, listed in order with novellas):

**Kibbles and Bits**: Sample the first stories in the series before you buy. The Fairies Saga stories. Find out how the first five books got their crazy names, too.

**Naked in the Winter Wind**: (lengthy novel) How does an older woman wind up as a young hottie in Revolutionary War era North Carolina? First book in the time travel series.

**Ha'Penny Jenny**: (historical novella) More about the naïve and psychic young girl who was adopted into a time traveling family. Will her past catch up to her?

**Aye, I am a Fairy**: (lengthy novel) Young British lord finds himself entwined with a time traveling family and must decide if he should go back in time, too. Second book in the series.

**Dances Naked**: (novel) Directionally challenged time traveler is rescued by Cherokee in 18th century. What must he do before the chief will show him to The Trees, the portal through time?

**Chasing Christmas**: (historical novella) A young Cherokee is rescued from an abusive man and changes the lives of many in this 18th century America family.

**The Great Big Fairy**: (lengthy novel) Very tall Benji grew up in the 20th century but was born in the 18th. When he finds a way to return to his grandparents in the distant past, he goes for it. Once there, he realizes he can't stay, but must return to the future. Fourth book in the series.

**Little Bear and the Ladies**: (historical novella) What's a bachelor trapper to do with all the females he rescues from the Hessian mercenaries? He'd better hurry and figure something!

**Little Drummer Boy**: (historical novella) Young Scout works to earn money for a home in post-Revolutionary War America but runs up against prejudices and snowstorms.

**Never Too Young**: (historical novella) Scout and Ha'Penny Jenny have grown up, but will they be able to spend their life together, or will the past and ruffians get in their way?

**Time in a Little Blue Bottle:** (time travel 'mash up' novella) Elvis, Mark Twain, and the prime vampire are racing to get the bottle of Fountain of Youth water before sweet Bella and the youthful pickpocket. So why are time travelers Marty Melbourne and Master Simon interested?

## CONTEMPORARY NOVELLAS – BENJI, THE LOST YEARS

**Luke the Unexpected**: Love of classic motorcycles brought them together, but Luke and Holly have other challenges to face. Find out how their friend Benji got his stripes here.

**Pool Boy Wanted: No Experience Preferred:** (rather racy) Young Benji has been a hostage and slave, but life gets worse when an older woman decides she wants him as her own.

## STAND ALONE NOVELLAS
### (contemporary romances)

**Kit Kringle: An Alaskan Tale:** Kay moved to Alaska for the wrong reasons, then decided to stay and start her own business. What she hadn't planned on were prejudices and falling in love.

**Be My Angel**: Wyatt's dream to help save the wild mustangs began with the purchase of a rundown ranch in western Oregon. What he hadn't anticipated was being mesmerized by a sassy woman in a wheelchair.

**Three Are One**: The post chaplain tried to help the young widow adjust, but would his feelings for her and the search for his lost sister cause problems?

**One Arctic Summer**: That unforgettable summer of 1994 in Barrow,

Alaska, and the touch she never forgot…If she goes back, will he remember her?

**The Polar Xpress:** Will the California chiropractor get a first chance at romance with the owner of Second Chance Kennels when he is stranded in Alaska?

# About the Author

USA Today bestselling author and entrepreneur Dani Haviland started writing late in life and has been making up for lost time with a torrential flood of romances. Tackling everything from historicals to suspense to paranormal themes—and sometimes smashing them together—she even tossed a rejuvenated Elvis into one story (Time in a Little Blue Bottle) to give it a little peanut butter crunch! Savor them all but start now. More are coming, and you don't want to get too far behind!

**Contact information:**

Email: **dani@danihaviland.com**

Twitter: **@dani_haviland**

*I love to hear from readers!*

Sign up for my newsletter to get the latest information on new releases, free stuff, and contests at: **http://bit.ly/2DHnews**

*Awesome readers make up a street team!*

I have a Facebook Page for folks who are interested in early excerpts and insights into my latest books and box sets. I'd appreciate a like on the page. Drop in and see if I've remembered to add photos and excerpts of my works in process. **http://bit.ly/2DaniStTeam**

www.ingramcontent.com/pod-product-compliance
Lightning Source LLC
Chambersburg PA
CBHW082010170626

46817CB00009B/3050